THE CLOCKWORK CROW

CATHERINE FISHER

WALKER BOOKS

First US paperback edition 2021
First published by Firefly Press (UK) 2018

Library of Congress Catalog Card Number 2020915498
ISBN 978-1-5362-1491-8 (hardcover)
ISBN 978-1-5362-2292-0 (paperback)

21 22 23 24 25 26 TRC 10 9 8 7 6 5 4 3 2 1

Printed in Eagan, MN, USA

This book was typeset in Manticore.

Walker Books US
a division of
Candlewick Press
99 Dover Street
Somerville, Massachusetts 02144

www.walkerbooksus.com

CONTENTS

SEREN RHYS IS FREEZING

A clock ticks, frost is white.
Stars travel through the night.

The railway station was deserted. The only thing that moved in its silent shadows was the big hand on the clock as it crept toward the hour of eight.

Seren stared up at it, hypnotized and weary. How could it go so slowly? Had she really only been waiting half an hour? It seemed like forever.

She was bundled in a heavy coat, a woolen hat, scarves, and a shawl, but she had never been colder in all her life. Even with thick gloves thrust deep in her pockets, she couldn't feel her fingers. Her toes were numb. In fact, if she didn't move right now, she would probably freeze on the spot, so she jumped to her feet and began to stamp up and down the bare platform, the thump of her clumsy boots ringing in the bitter night.

She stamped fourteen steps to the wall.

Fourteen steps back.

To the wall.

And back.

Over everything—the benches and the roof and the railway posters—a thin layer of frost shimmered like crushed diamonds in the light from the lamp. The night was so silent it scared her. She breathed out a cloud and then turned quickly as the stationmaster's door opened. A big man in uniform came out and stared at her.

"Are you on your own, miss?"

It was a ridiculous question and it annoyed her. There were a lot of cross answers she could have snapped out, but she swallowed them and just said, "Yes."

"Waiting for the eight forty, are you?"

"Is there any other train?"

"Well, no. Not this time of night."

He was a red-faced man, and he wore a peaked cap that looked as if it had been sat on more than once. He stared down at her, as if she puzzled him. Finally he said, "It's an unusually cold night. You could go in the waiting room, but it's First Class. Are you First Class?"

She knew she wasn't. No one ever spent that sort of money on her, but she pulled out her ticket and looked at it. THIRD it said, in large letters. She put it back in her pocket before he could see it, drew herself up, and said, "Yes. That's right. First Class. Show me the waiting room, please."

For a moment, she thought he didn't believe her. Maybe he didn't, but he smiled, picked up her suitcase, and set off along the platform. The case looked tiny in his hand, even though she had found it so heavy. She hurried after him to a door with FIRST CLASS WAITING ROOM written on the frosted glass; he opened it and said, "Here we go. This'll be a bit cozier. You'll be like toast in here till the train comes."

She pushed past him into a warmth that was so wonderful, she wanted to shout with sheer relief.

The room was small; there was a bench against each wall, a big table with an oil lamp on it, and best of all, a fire in the grate, a pile of coals glowing scarlet under a coat of ashes.

She went straight across and huddled over it.

"You're nearly frozen." The stationmaster stepped back and looked at her curiously. "I haven't seen you around here before. Traveled a long way, have you?"

"I used to live in India."

"Blimey! I expect it was hotter there?"

Despite herself, she allowed a tiny smile. "A bit."

"Couldn't stand that myself. All them flies and mosquitoes and tigers. Now, you sit down and make yourself comfortable. No one to disturb you. You'll hear the train easy enough."

He went out, letting in a shiver of icy air. Seren pulled off her gloves and found her fingers were blue and numb. She dragged the heavy bench closer to the coals and sat on it, tucking her feet up and pulling her coat and shawl tighter around her.

This was so much better! Warmth began to thaw out her nose and ears and fingers; it was painful, but worth it. She yawned, wishing she could go to sleep, but she had to be careful not to miss the train.

The fire crackled and she watched it. Of course what she had told the stationmaster about India was true—she had lived there once, but only as a tiny baby. She couldn't remember anything about it at all, really, except a sort of vagueness of heat and the fierce blue glare of the sky.

And someone leaning over her, and kissing her.

She shrugged it away. Her parents had both died out there, and she had been brought home on the ship and had lived for twelve years at the orphanage of St. Mary's. Even now, she couldn't believe she was out of that place. Her great-aunt Grace had found her and taken her away, but only for six months, because now Aunt Grace was dead, too. The old woman had been bedridden, living in lonely splendor at the top of a dull old house near London, and Seren had hardly seen her. She had stayed in the kitchen mostly, with Martha the maid and the white cat, Samuel. She was already missing them; maybe there would be a cat at Plas-y-Fran.

In her pocket the letter crackled; she took it out and moved nearer to the lamp to read it again.

Dear Seren,

Here is your railway ticket. As I told you at your aunt's funeral, your father's oldest friend, Captain Arthur Jones, has offered to take you in. Captain Jones is your godfather. It seems strange you have never met him. He has a wife—Lady Mair—and one son, called Tomos, and his house is in Wales. It's a grand old place, called Plas-y-Fran. The train will take you to Trefil, the nearest station, where I'm sure someone will come to meet you.

I hope you will be happy living there.

Yours, most sincerely,
G. R. Freeman
Solicitor at Law
Staple Inn
London

Seren crumpled it up thoughtfully. A grand house! She hugged her knees and dreamed. There would certainly be a hot bath and a huge bedroom with curtains around the bed. There would be maids and footmen and glittering chandeliers and delicious cakes. New clothes for sure. And Captain Jones would be a tall, handsome man with a mustache, and Lady Mair would be pretty, and they would be waiting anxiously on the doorstep to meet her. And there was a boy in the house! Master Tomos. She imagined him with dark hair and a clever, cheerful face, holding out his hand and saying, "Hello, Seren, it's so great you're here!"

It seemed too good to be true.

But maybe it was. Maybe this Tomos was some spoiled little brat who would resent her coming and they would argue and he would pull her hair. Well, let him try!

She yawned again. The fire crackled, so quiet and warm that she closed her eyes. For a moment, everything was peaceful.

Then somebody coughed.

It was a soft sound, the very smallest sound. But it made her snap her eyes open in alarm. She stared across the table and sat bolt upright in shock.

There was a man in the room!

He was leaning back in the shadowy corner of the bench opposite her, all the way back in the dark, so she could barely see him. A very tall, thin man with clothes as black as midnight. He wore a hat that hid his eyes, though she knew he was looking at her. On his lap was a large parcel, wrapped in newspaper and tied with string. He held it tight with both hands; his fingers were long and spindly, and on one was a ring, its stone a green glimmer of emerald.

Seren sat frozen in complete shock. Where on earth had he come from?

He couldn't have been here the whole time. The room had been empty. The door had never opened. And even if she'd fallen asleep, it could only have been for a second.

"Hello," the man said quietly.

"Hello," she said, to be polite. She looked down and saw her fingers were twisted together. She uncurled her legs and sat up straight. What was there to be scared of? It was a waiting room. Anyone could come in and wait. But still, she didn't like it.

A coal slid in the fire.

The man's voice was not much more than a whisper. "Are you waiting for a train?"

"Yes."

He sat upright. He seemed very restless. "So am I. Maybe it's the same one. But it's late—I'm sure it's late."

He didn't seem very frightening after all. She had never seen anyone so thin or so anxious.

"It's not due yet," she said.

He glanced over quickly at the door, and she saw his eyes, dark and wary, lit by a slant of lamplight from outside. "Did you hear that?"

She stared at him. "Hear what?"

"That . . . *Listen!*"

She listened. She heard the wind. The tick of the clock. And maybe a distant drift of sound, like a far-off cry.

The effect on the man was astonishing. He jumped up in panic. "It's Them! I'm sure it's Them. Do you think we can lock the door?" He hurried over to it. But there was no key, so he opened it a slit and peered out. "I can't see anything. It's so dark!"

He came back. Too agitated to sit, he paced up and down.

Such a tall man. Seren watched him, fascinated. His hands, clutching the parcel, were long and fine, like the hands of a prince in one of her books. Whatever he had in there must be precious; he held it so tight against himself, the newspaper crackled.

No one came in. Only the wind whispered at the door. Seren wished the big red-faced stationmaster would come back, but there was no sign of him.

Then, quite clearly, she heard it again. Nearer now. A strange cry, cold and sharp and angry. As if some arctic bird circled high in the frosty night.

The stranger gave a murmur of terror and stood still.

He put his face right up against the window and looked out, but there was only blackness. Seren could see the reflection of his face, white and weary-looking under the tilted hat. Then he pulled down the blind and turned, so fast it made her jump.

"You heard that!"

"Yes," she said. "Is it a gull?"

His laugh was hollow. "No, it's not a gull. I wish it was . . . Look . . ." He glanced down at the parcel, then at her, sharply. "I have to go out there. I have to see if it's Them. Can I trust you?"

She shrugged. "Well, yes, but I don't—"

"Are you an honest girl? You look as if you are." With a sudden, decisive movement, he held the parcel out. "I need you to look after this. Just for a moment."

"But my train!"

"I won't be long. Don't you understand? I don't dare take it out there in case. They'll see it! A few moments, that's all. Please."

Reluctantly, she took it. He seemed hugely relieved. "Don't move. I'll be right back." He was already at the door, but before he ran out, he turned, his long fingers grasping the wooden panel. His voice was an anguish of worry. "If They get me, whatever happens, *don't leave it here alone.* Promise me?"

Astonished, she nodded.

Then he was gone.

Seren looked down at the parcel in her hands. It was heavy, and as big as a loaf of bread. For a moment she thought something inside it croaked. It startled her so much, she dropped it quickly onto the table and sat down, but her peace was shattered and she felt scared and edgy.

The clock ticked time away. One minute.

Two.

Five.

Ten.

He didn't come back.

She stood up and hurried to the door, opening it and peering out. "Hello?" she said. "Are you there?"

But the station was silent and icy.

By 8:40, he still hadn't returned. Seren stood by the table, staring at the paper parcel. What if her train came?

At once, as if she had summoned it, a shrill whistle split the night.

.·*★.➤*·. 11 ..*✦.·*.

What should she do? Leave the parcel here where anyone might steal it? Call the stationmaster? Yes! That would be best!

She grabbed her suitcase and hauled it toward the door.

The train was already rumbling in from the darkness and settling to a long, hissing stop, its cars and engine clicking and sparking with heat. Brakes screeched. Steam erupted in billowy clouds. The air was sharp with the stink of oil and coal.

Doors swung open. Passengers climbed down.

All at once, the station was full of people chattering, calling out, unloading bags; she looked hurriedly for the stationmaster, but he was far down at the end with his back to her, supervising great milk churns being loaded on.

"Excuse me!" Seren yelled. "Hey! *Hello!*"

He couldn't hear her. She looked around. The thin stranger was still nowhere to be seen. But it wasn't her business, was it, any of this? She just had to get on the train, so she tugged one of the car doors open and climbed up, dragging her heavy suitcase inside and dumping it with relief on the faded red seat.

Then she leaned out of the door, hanging on tight.

Across the platform, the waiting room was softly lamplit. She could see the newspaper parcel, lying abandoned and unprotected on the table.

She waved wildly. "Hey! Can you hear me?"

Far off, the stationmaster blew his whistle. He waved back and raised a green flag.

Whatever happens, don't leave it here alone the stranger had said. More than said. Begged. As if whatever was in there was precious.

She had to do something.

In an instant, she jumped down, raced across the platform, dived into the waiting room, snatched the parcel, and ran out with it. The train was already moving; she ran alongside it and grabbed the rail.

Somebody shouted in alarm. For a terrifying moment, she knew she was being whisked off her feet, then she scrambled up the steps and flung herself inside, the heavy door slamming. The whistle gave a great screech as she fell on the dirty floor with the parcel under her.

Sparks flew past the window.

The station was already half a mile behind.

The train roared away into the night.

THE NEWSPAPER PARCEL

Hidden in my paper stars,
Carry me to where you are.

Seren picked herself up and collapsed on the seat. She was breathless and sore. Not only that, but her coat—her only coat!—was all spattered with smudges of soot. Probably her face was, too. Furious, she threw the newspaper parcel down, pulled out a handkerchief, and tried to clean herself, but it was hopeless. The dirt just smeared and got worse.

And she'd wanted to arrive looking so sharp!

She scrunched the handkerchief up and stared in dismay at the parcel. What on earth was she going to do with this? As the train rattled, the whole car swayed and the package slid slightly on the seat.

She'd just have to give it to someone at Trefil station. Hand it in as lost property. Then she'd be rid of it and the owner could come and get it.

Once she'd decided on a plan, she felt a lot better. She leaned back in her seat and looked at the window, but she could only see herself reflected, small and scruffy, and the compartment with its two pictures of donkeys at the shore in the flickering gaslight.

She sighed. How far was it to Trefil? Probably ages. And she was so hungry!

Looking at the parcel, she noticed that one corner of the newspaper had been torn in her struggle to get on board. Something small and shiny was glinting inside there. Something as brilliant as a jewel.

Seren tapped her fingers on the table. She shouldn't really be nosy. It wasn't hers, after all. But then curiosity became too much, and, because there was no harm in just looking, she leaned forward and began, very carefully, to untie the string that held the whole thing together.

The knots were tight. In the end, she had to take her gloves off and pick at them with her nails, but finally she managed to pry the last one loose, and the string fell away.

She pulled the newspaper apart.

The parcel was open, and its contents were baffling.

Cogs and wheels, pins and screws. A pile of small springs. Something that looked like a beak, hinged with leather. A great mass of black feathers. Two sharp talons and a higgledy-piggledy heap of what might be pieces of wing.

She examined it all carefully with her cold fingers.

Right at the bottom, looking up at her sideways, was the shiny jewel. She saw now that it was blue, shaped like an eye, cut from purest crystal. There was another, too; it rolled along the table as the train lurched, and she grabbed at it. As she picked it up, it must have caught some gleam of light from outside, because for a moment, it sparkled and winked at her like a tiny star.

"What are you?" she whispered.

The train rattled. She put the jewel down and saw, folded inside the parcel, a piece of white paper. She opened it and a key fell out. She read the words on the paper.

THE CLOCKWORK CROW
Danger!
DO NOT ASSEMBLE
*For the journey is long and the road leads
into darkness.*

So it was some sort of toy. A puzzle? What good
was it if you couldn't assemble it? She felt oddly disappointed. That man in the dark coat had been really
scared and desperate to keep this safe, but why was a
toy so important? Was it a present for his little boy?
That might be it, because soon it would be Christmas.

She put the paper down and leaned back, closing
her eyes and thinking about how Christmas would
be at Plas-y-Fran. There was bound to be a huge tree
full of shining candles, and a goose to eat, plum pud-
ding, and maybe oranges. And a present all wrapped in
shiny gold paper that Lady Mair would hold out to her.
"This is for you, Seren, with our love." Inside there would
be the sweetest silver chain, with a tiny crescent moon
sparkling on the end of it.

At the orphanage, Christmas had been very dull.
Every year, she'd had only a small packet of handkerchiefs

embroidered with a curly letter S for a present. The only real Christmas trees she had ever seen had been in the windows of a big London shop—Martha had taken her down there one evening, and how the trees had glittered and shone, hung with striped canes of gingerbread!

Half-asleep, she let herself fall into a lovely dream of dresses and toys, until with a small *plip*, as if the gas had run out, the lamp above her went off and she was in complete darkness.

Now she could see outside. There was a moon, a thin fingernail over the hills, and it shone on a strange, mountainous country. She had never seen such great hills, such deep wooded valleys. The silver light flickered on a waterfall, crashing through dark branches.

So this was Wales.

It looked wild, she thought. A little scary.

Brakes hissed. The train began to slow. Hurriedly, Seren gathered all the pieces of the black toy and swept them into the parcel, fumbling with the knots, but she had no time to tie them together properly before the train had rumbled to a halt. There outside the window, in white letters on a black iron sign, was the word TREFIL.

She grabbed her suitcase and flung open the door.

It was bitterly cold. Jumping down, she tugged the suitcase out and, with the parcel under her arm, turned to find the stationmaster.

The train huffed and blew a great snort of steam. It began to move off, slowly at first, then faster and faster until for a moment, she was completely lost in the smoke, as if a cloud had come down and enveloped her or a huge invisible dragon had breathed fire all around her.

Then it cleared, the deafening noise died away, and the train was gone.

She was alone.

There was no station. Just a bare platform under some overhanging trees. Stars shone overhead with frosty brilliance.

There was no stationmaster, no waiting room, not even a building.

So what could she do with the parcel?

Heaving up her suitcase, she hobbled to the fence and through a tiny gate. In the darkness, something whickered; she sensed rather than saw a horse and, behind it, the dark shadow of a carriage. Someone said, "The little girl for the Plas, is it?"

"Yes." She peered into the dark. "Who's there, please?"

He got down and came toward her, and she stepped back a little in surprise, because he was the smallest man she had ever seen. The whip in his hand was nearly as tall as he was. Eye to eye, he looked at her. "I'm Denzil," he said.

She glanced around.

The night was a silvery silence, though the bare trees made a soft swish in the breeze. There were no lights and no sign of anyone else in this dark lane.

The small man didn't wait for a reply. He picked up her suitcase and lugged it to the carriage. "This is far too heavy," he said. "What's in it?"

Seren was immediately annoyed. What business was it of his? "My books," she said haughtily.

He laughed, a short bark of scorn. "Books! There's plenty of books at the Plas, and no one to read them, either." Opening the door, he thrust the case in, then beckoned her with an impatient hand. "Come *on*, girl! Or it'll be past midnight before we get to our beds."

She took a step toward the carriage. The parcel! But there was no one to leave it with, and besides, she was too cold and tired now to think, so she gave up and climbed the step into the dark interior. Denzil fastened the door on her at once.

She heard him clamber up, flick the reins, and say "Whup!" and the carriage began to jolt.

It was very black in here. She put her hand out and felt the seat; it was soft and well padded. And then her hand touched wool and found a folded blanket. She opened it gratefully and tugged it around her shoulders.

It helped. But the carriage smelled of damp and mold, as if it was never used, and that was surprising. And the roads must be awful, because the jolting swung her from side to side until she had to hang on to the leather strap by the window.

She kept the parcel on her lap. After all, she was responsible for it now. It was a real nuisance, and she was starting to hate it. She wished she'd never even picked up the thing, but there was nothing she could do about that except try not to think about the thin man in the dark hat, searching desperately for his lost clockwork toy.

The carriage rumbled uphill and downhill. Branches brushed against it, brittle twigs snapping against the roof. The jolting made her feel sick. She gritted her teeth and told herself firmly that it was all right, because very soon now, there would be the big house with its blaze of windows, and Captain Arthur Jones and Lady Mair waiting on the doorstep for her, maybe with Tomos, though Tomos should be already tucked in bed. They would take her into a glorious parlor hung with blue satin and hug her and say, "*Welcome, Seren. This is your home now.*"

It was a dream she had dreamed many times in the orphanage, curled up in bed when the room was quiet. Only the moon, peering in through the window, had shared her dream. Now it was really coming true. But her eyes were heavy, and she couldn't stop yawning.

The coach slowed. The shadow of a great gate swung past her; for a moment, she saw a pillar, crowned with the silhouette of a stone eagle against the stars. At last! They were here.

She pushed back the flimsy curtain, tugged down the window, and stared out.

Under the moonlight she saw a great crag, and

beside it a lake, shining like a silver mirror. On the lakeside rose the turrets and gables of an ancient house.

Seren stared, amazed. It was so much bigger than she'd imagined. It looked like a castle, or maybe an asylum. As the carriage rattled toward it, she saw that ivy covered the roof, and a few dark birds flitted high above the battlements.

But the building was in complete darkness. There were no lights at the windows. It had an empty, ghostly look about it that made her uneasy.

The carriage rattled under another archway and into a cobbled yard where the wheels made such a racket, it should have woken everyone. But when the carriage stopped, there was a frozen silence, until the door was yanked open and the tiny man stood there looking up at her.

"We're here. Get down, then."

Seren climbed down. He tugged her suitcase after her. "Watch your step. Bit mucky here."

In the stone wall of the house was a door; he opened it, and a shaft of moonlight showed her a corridor, stone-flagged and shadowy.

The small man marched along it and Seren followed,

hurrying to keep up. Why had no one been waiting for her? But of course, it was a freezing night! They'd all be inside by some warm fireplace, listening anxiously for the coach. The thought made her feel better, but still, there was something wrong about the place. Small oil lamps lit the walls, throwing a mass of shadows; the corridor turned right and left, past closed doors. It smelled musty, and the only sound was the shuffling of her feet and Denzil's mutterings and puffings. Finally, the small man came to a green-painted door; he turned the handle and led her in. "This is it."

Seren stood still in dismay.

It was a kitchen, but it was nothing like the cozy space she had imagined.

It was huge and bare. A vast sooty chimney opened in the wall, and the fire that smoldered below was almost out. In a chair next to it, a woman in a dark dress was sewing, but as soon as she saw Seren, she tossed the embroidery aside and stood up. She was very tall. Her face was hard and stern.

"So," she said. "You're here at last! Have you any idea how late you are?"

Seren bobbed a curtsy because that was what they

taught you at the orphanage. But she was really worried now. Surely this couldn't be Lady Mair?

"The train was late," she muttered.

The woman frowned in distaste. She walked right around Seren, looking at her closely. The hem of her dress swished the dust on the floor. She didn't bend down or even smile. Her gloved hands were clasped together, and her face was narrow, her lips tight, her eyes gray and disapproving. "You will please address me as Ma'am. Is that suitcase your luggage? It seems a lot for a small girl."

"My books are in there. Ma'am."

"Really? I had no idea you were allowed such things. There are plenty of books here."

"So I'm told," Seren growled.

"She'll be hungry," Denzil said.

"I'm sure she will. Children always are." The tall woman frowned. "My name is Mrs. Villiers. I am the housekeeper here."

Seren looked around. "I suppose Captain Jones and his family are all in bed?"

The housekeeper gave Denzil a quick glance. He shrugged and left the room.

"We'll discuss that tomorrow," Mrs. Villiers said quickly. "Now, eat your supper."

She pointed to the table. On one end was a plate of sandwiches. They had been waiting so long that their corners were dry and curled up, and they were only canned meat, but Seren sat and ate them fast because she was too hungry to be fussy. She was still hungry when she'd finished, but it was clear there would be no more.

Mrs. Villiers poured tea, hot and strong, from a big brown pot. Seren gulped it down, even though it scorched her mouth.

She wanted to ask a lot more questions, but even before she had finished the tea, Mrs. Villiers had whisked the plate and cup away and was standing over her with a lighted candle. "Come on now, quickly. No dawdling! Stay close to me. This is an old house and it's easy to get lost."

Seren looked around. Denzil must have taken her suitcase, but the newspaper parcel lay on a chair.

She picked it up.

"What is that?" Mrs. Villiers demanded.

Seren shrugged. Suddenly she didn't want to say. "Something private."

The housekeeper shook her head. "Let me see." She snatched it away, pulled the paper open, and looked inside. "What on earth . . . ?"

"It's a toy." Seren had a sudden idea. "My great-aunt gave it to me." She cast her eyes down sadly. "It's all I have to remind me of her."

It worked. Mrs. Villiers snorted, thrust the parcel back at her, and pushed her to the door.

Stumbling, as weary as if she were walking through a dream, Seren followed. The house was enormous. She sleepwalked along dark corridors, up vast flights of stairs, through curtained alcoves, Mrs. Villiers stalking ahead with the candle held high. She had a dim sense of many rooms, of dark portraits on the walls, of cabinets glimmering with glass and china. The air was so musty, it was hard to breathe.

Finally, Mrs. Villiers came to a white-painted corridor and threw open a door.

"This is your room. There's water for washing in the jug. Breakfast is at eight. Please don't be late."

Then she turned and walked away, taking the light with her.

"Good night," Seren said.

.*★.➤.*·· 27 ··*.◡.*★

Mrs. Villiers turned, a little surprised. But she said, "Good night."

Seren went in and looked around. The room was dim and shadowy, with dark masses of furniture. She dumped the parcel on a table. The bed was very high and it had curtains all around it. She opened them and crawled inside. Instantly, without washing, or even taking her coat off, she fell asleep.

She almost woke once, deep in the night, thinking she heard the high, sweet note of a bell, silvery and sharp.

But it might have been a dream.

THE SILENCE OF THE HOUSE

Down the stairs, in the rooms,
Shadows whisper of their dreams.

In the morning the breakfast bell woke her.

Seren lay warm under the sheets. At some point in the night, she had pulled her coat off, but her dress was a mess and her hair a wild tangle. For a moment she stayed there, curled up, remembering the train and the thin man, the bitter cold, and the carriage ride through the hills. Then she slid down from the bed and ran to the window, throwing the dusty curtains wide.

She saw an expanse of frosted lawns. Beyond, the bare branches of a wood rose against a leaden sky. The wood surrounded the house, and the winter trees were stark in the gray morning. Everything was still, but then some swans flew over the house with a whistling of wings, and she remembered that there was a lake down there among the trees.

It all looked bitterly cold.

Still, it was time for breakfast, and she was starving!

She unpacked her other dress, the blue one, and stepped into it. She dragged a comb through her hair. She had to look sharp to meet the captain and Lady Mair. And Tomos.

The small clock by her bed said five minutes past eight, so she was already late.

She opened the door and peered out. The corridor was empty. Seren ran along it and down some twisty stairs; last night she had been too tired to take much notice, but now she was alert and interested in every detail of the house.

At the bottom was a wider corridor, lined with cabinets of china and glass, some of the plates and jugs so large they reflected her face in warped and delicate glances. The floorboards creaked loudly, but there was no other sound. Just like last night, the air of the house seemed muffled, as if no one breathed it. Everywhere was cold. The windows were shuttered. She was starting to think she might wander here forever when she came to a large hall, its furniture covered with white sheets. Where was everyone? It wasn't right, all this silence. Puzzled, she ran past mirrors, a dusty dining table, cobwebbed chairs, through a blue room, a red room, and a room with yellow silk hangings, until finally she found the corridor that led to the kitchen.

At last she heard the sound of people—a clatter of dishes, a murmur of voices. The smell of toasted bread and warm milk drifted out, so she walked quickly down there and peeked around the door.

There was a cat! A white cat!

He had already turned his head and was staring at her, and his eyes were green. He got up, stretched, and stalked over, arching his back as she smoothed his soft, warm fur.

Mrs. Villiers was standing at the fireside. She said, "Didn't you hear the bell?"

"I got lost. It's such a huge house." Seren laughed as the cat rolled over elegantly on the flagstones. "What's his name?"

"I did tell you to please address me as Ma'am."

"His name's Sam." It was Denzil who answered. He was sitting at the big wooden table with a pile of potatoes in front of him, peeling them with a sharp knife. Seren came over and stood beside him.

"Sit here." Mrs. Villiers pointed to a chair. She pulled a pot from the fire and scooped porridge into a bowl. She put it on the table with a wooden spoon and a cup for tea.

Seren came and sat. The chair was a child's chair, a bit small for her. She ate quickly, looking around.

The kitchen wasn't quite as bare as she'd first thought. Hanging on hooks high up under the rafters was a great row of copper pots and pans, starting with tiny little jugs and getting bigger until the last one was so huge and heavy, she could easily have climbed inside it.

The porridge was sweet and gloopy, but better than at St. Mary's. Gulping it down, she said, "So where is everyone? The family and the servants? I really want to say hello to Tomos."

There was a tight silence.

Mrs. Villiers sat opposite her. She looked as if she had been waiting for the question. She folded her fingers together on the tabletop and said firmly, "We are the only people in the house at the moment."

"Just us?"

"And the cook, Alys, who comes in from the village at lunchtime."

"No one else?"

"Gwyn," Denzil muttered.

Mrs. Villiers glared at him. "Gwyn is a gardener's boy. He's not house staff."

Denzil shrugged.

Astonished, Seren licked the spoon and dumped it in the dish. "But . . . I thought Captain Jones . . ."

"Captain Jones is away. In London, I believe."

"And Lady Mair?"

"Lady Mair is in London, too."

It was hugely disappointing. "Will they come home for Christmas?"

This silence was even worse. She knew at once that she had said something dreadful. Denzil's knife stopped scraping, just for a second, then resumed with a fierce intensity.

Mrs. Villiers stood, turned her back, and speared a piece of bread on a fork. "No. They won't. I'm afraid, Seren, that life in Plas-y-Fran might not be quite what you were expecting. The family is not here, and where they are and what they do is none of your business. It will be rather lonely for you, because obviously you will not be able to mix with the village children . . ."

"Why not? What's wrong with them?" Seren asked.

Denzil snorted a laugh. Mrs. Villiers gave him an irritated stare. "Nothing . . . But you are part of this household now and . . ."

Seren was suddenly annoyed, too. It was all so different from what she'd dreamed of. "But there *is* no household. No one to talk to and no one to play with."

Mrs. Villiers drew herself up. "Please don't talk to me in that impudent fashion. I don't know how you behaved at the orphanage, but . . ."

"Well, at least there were other people there. And lessons." Seren looked up with a sudden fear. "I mean, I will have lessons, won't I? A tutor, or a school?"

"You *like* lessons?" Denzil sounded amazed.

"Yes, of course."

"That's not like a child."

"Rubbish," she snapped.

Mrs. Villiers stared. "*What* did you say?"

"Well, I'm sorry—Ma'am—but it is. Why shouldn't children like learning? Besides, I'm going to be a great writer one day, so I need to learn everything I can."

Denzil blinked and sliced another potato. "If you say so."

There was silence for a moment. Seren scratched her nose. Then she asked, "Where can I go?"

Mrs. Villiers looked even more astonished. "Go?"

"To explore. Can I go anywhere on the grounds? In the house?" Then, because she was so irritated she couldn't help it, she got up and paced around. "I'm sorry, but it's all so strange here! Such a big house and no one in it, and I was really hoping . . ." She stopped, because all at once her dreams seemed silly. She should have known no one would care about her.

"You won't be bored, if that's what's worrying you." Denzil stabbed the knife into the table as if he was angry, and it stood upright. "There's an enormous library upstairs, crammed with books, and there's a nursery full of . . ."

He stopped. Mrs. Villiers had put her white fingers on his wrist. In a quiet voice, not meant for Seren to hear, she whispered, "Hush."

Then she turned to Seren. "Sit down."

Seren folded her arms. But she sat.

"Now listen to me. These are the rules. You can walk anywhere you wish in the gardens—there are pretty paths and seats there. But you do not go through the iron gate that leads into the parkland or anywhere near the lake. Is that clear?"

Seren nodded, stubborn. She should have known there would be rules.

"Answer me, please."

"Yes, Mrs. Villiers."

"As for the house, you may visit the lower rooms, though most of them are closed up for the winter. You may use the library. But you do *not* go up the top staircase into the attic."

It was all so miserable! Seren tangled a curl of hair around her finger. Then she blurted out the question that had been tormenting her all along. "Mrs. Villiers, where's Tomos?"

This time, the silence was absolute, and a bit scary. She looked at Denzil. He stared at his empty hands. Mrs. Villiers got up and went to the fire.

Her voice was cold. "Tomos is not here."

"Is he in London? With his mother?"

Mrs. Villiers turned, and her face was white. "Master

Tomos is absolutely no business of yours. You are a very impudent, cheeky little girl."

That was unfair, Seren thought. She could feel herself going red, but before she could ask anything else, Mrs. Villiers came over, snatched away the breakfast dishes, and took them to the scullery. There was a loud rattle of crockery and an angry splash of water.

Seren looked at Denzil. "What did I say?"

He frowned. "Don't get upset, girl. Things are difficult here. If it was me, I would tell you, but . . ."

"Tell me what?"

But Mrs. Villiers was back. "Don't you have work to do, Denzil?"

He got up, jumping down from the high stool. Without another look at Seren, he went out, and the cat ran after him.

"Now. Stand up."

Seren stood in front of the tall woman.

"Is that your only dress?"

"My best one. I have one other."

"You have indoor shoes?"

"No. Just these boots."

Mrs. Villiers clicked her tongue. "Dear me. We

must get something done before Sunday. I can't have the villagers seeing such a tattered object in the Plas-y-Fran pew. When did you last wash your hair?"

Seren couldn't remember. "Last week?" she lied.

"It's a filthy tangle, and you probably have lice."

"No, I don't!"

"You will need a bath."

She was glad about that, as long as it wasn't icy cold. Mrs. Villiers said, "I'll have the water heated. In the meantime, go up to your room, unpack, and lay everything out tidily on the bed—I'll be coming up to inspect it immediately."

Ten minutes later, she picked up Seren's old gray petticoat and chemise with the ends of her fingers in disgust. "Good heavens! All this will have to be burned. I shall write to Lady Mair at once explaining you will need completely new clothes. Now, come with me."

To Seren's astonishment, the bath was not a tin tub in front of the fire, but a real white bath in a real bathroom, with big taps that turned and hot water that came out of them and steamed up to the marble ceiling. She stared at it all, wide-eyed in fascination.

"Make sure you scrub every inch." Mrs. Villiers

turned in the doorway, undecided. "Perhaps I should stay and supervise."

But the appalled look on Seren's face changed her mind. "Well . . . you are old enough to clean yourself. But I don't want a spot of dirt left on the bath, and the floor must be completely dry. Afterward, if you wish, you may explore the house. But remember you are *not* to go up to the top corridor, as there is nothing up there but the attic, and I do not want it disturbed. Is that clear?"

Seren sighed. "Yes, Mrs. Villiers."

But in a few minutes her sigh was of delight, because the water was warm and the soap smelled sweet. This was much more like it. This was luxury!

She lay back in the steamy heat and thought about what Mrs. Villiers had told her about the family.

Something was wrong. Something about Tomos.

She would certainly have to find out what it was.

A BRIGHT EYE

Claw and beak and wing and eye.
Wind me up and let me fly.

After her bath and back in her old dress, Seren sat in the window seat of her bedroom, looking gloomily out at the white lawns.

So no one else was here. No Sir Arthur and Lady Mair, no Tomos. But why had Mrs. Villiers been so strange about Tomos? She had seemed really angry. There was obviously some secret or Denzil wouldn't have said what he had. It was all very odd.

Then she thought of what it would mean for her. A lonely, dreary house, and all the long, empty winter days to come with just dull adults to talk to. And what sort of Christmas?

It made her feel so miserable that, just for a second, she wished she was back at St. Mary's, with its chilly dormitory and all the noisy girls, the horrible food, and the bare schoolroom.

But no.

That was nonsense.

Because here she had a whole house to herself. It was like a palace. And she was the princess.

Looking around at the fine bed and the wardrobe, the shelf with her few precious books arranged in a row, she felt happier.

Until her eye fell on the newspaper parcel and she groaned aloud.

She had to do something about that!

She went downstairs and tried every room until she found the library. Peering around the door, she saw it was cold and dark, but when she pulled back one of the high curtains to let in some light, she stared in awe at the hundreds and hundreds of books lining the wooden cabinets. Denzil was right. She certainly had plenty to read.

In a drawer, she found what she needed—a pencil and some paper—and wrote a note. It said:

Dear Sir,

If a tall thin man comes looking for a newspaper
parsel containing a clockwork toy, could you please
give him my adress and ask him to call here for
it? I am sorry I took it by mistake.

Yours sinserely
Seren Rhys

She frowned. Maybe there were a few spelling mis-
takes. But it wouldn't matter.

She put it in an envelope and addressed it to:

THE STATION MASTER
CASTLE HOLLOW STATION
WALES

That should be enough to get it to the right place.
She sealed it with wax and took the letter down to
the hall—she was starting to find her way a bit more
easily now—and saw Denzil on his hands and knees
scrubbing the tiled floor. He certainly seemed to have

plenty of work to do. She stood looking down at him a moment, then said, "How do I mail this?"

He sloshed water, hot and breathless. "What is it?"

"A letter."

"Leave it in the postbox there on the table. I'll take it in with the kitchen orders this afternoon." Watching her put it in the box, he said, "So who are you writing to, then, little orphan?"

She shrugged. "That's private."

He grinned and went back to scrubbing; the brush rasped hard on the bare tiles. After a while, she said, "Do you do all the work?"

"Someone has to."

"Where are all the servants?"

"Sent away," he said.

It would take a lot of work to keep a house this size clean. Why send the servants away? Seren put her hands in her pockets; she wanted to ask more, but she sensed he was already cross. But there was something else, something that had popped from nowhere into her memory.

"Denzil. Did a clock strike, late in the night?"

"The stable clock strikes every hour."

"No, not that, that's loud, like a clang. This was something . . . silvery. Sort of icy. I think it was inside the house."

The brush stopped scrubbing.

For a moment he was still, then he looked up. She thought he looked scared. He said, "There's no bell like that here. Dreaming, you were."

"Maybe." She wandered off, but at the turn of the corridor, she stopped and peeked back.

He was kneeling, staring into space, and the brush was lying forgotten in a pool of water.

Seren spent the rest of the day exploring. There were so many rooms in the great house, she lost count of them, but everywhere was the same: dreary and dark, the windows shuttered and the furniture covered with white dust sheets. She peeked under some of these and found delicate tables and mahogany cupboards that would have looked lovely all polished in candlelight. She spent a while staring up at the rows of portraits on the stairs, faces of men and women long dead, gazing down at her. Most of them were old, but two were new. One showed a tall man with sandy hair; he wore a red uniform with gold braid on his shoulders, and was riding a great black horse.

Underneath, it said CAPTAIN ARTHUR JONES.

So this was him! He really did have a mustache.

Next to him, sitting in a chair with a small dog on her lap, was LADY MAIR JONES, and Seren saw she was pretty, with long dark hair and laughing eyes, and her dress was of green velvet and lace.

They looked nice. She so wished they were here.

There was no picture of Tomos.

Finally, after an hour, Seren had explored everywhere. All that was left was the small stairway to the attic. She walked to the bottom and looked up. Mrs. Villiers had been very clear. *Don't go up to the attic.* In fact, she had said it twice, and that was what was making Seren suspicious. What secret was kept up there?

She frowned and tapped her foot. If she were a real detective, like Mr. Sherlock Holmes, she would find out.

She looked around, but the house was silent. So she crept up the attic stairs.

At the top was a white-painted corridor, the ceiling very low. She tiptoed along it, opening the doors on each side, but every single room was empty, with absolutely nothing in them. The last door faced her at the end of the corridor. When she got to it, she turned the handle.

It was locked.

She crouched down, put her eye to the keyhole, and looked in.

She took a breath of delight. A nursery! She could see toys—there was a beautiful rocking horse with a long mane, some toy soldiers, and the corner of a puppet theater, all painted yellow and red.

It must be Tomos's room. If only she could get in.

She rattled the door again, but it was solid and unmoving. Why was just this room, out of all the rooms in the house, kept locked? What was so secret in there?

Inside the room, something dark crossed the light.

Seren jumped back.

Was there someone in there?

For a moment, she couldn't move. Then, very carefully, she crouched down and peered through again.

Had it been someone, or just a bird's shadow crossing the window? She could see the rocking horse again, and the puppet theater. Surely the horse was moving, just a tiny bit?

Very scared, she whispered, "Hello?"

There was no answer.

"Is anyone in there?" And then, "Tomos? Is that you?"

A small sound. She listened intently. Was there somebody breathing, just on the other side of the door? Or was it the wind, softly gusting under the roof?

Far below, the luncheon gong clanged.

She waited a moment. Then she whispered, "If anyone's there, my name is Seren. I've got to go now. But I'll be back."

Then she turned and ran.

All the way down the stairs, her heart thumped with excitement. Was it Tomos in there? If so, why was he locked up? She had to get into that nursery and see, just like Mr. Sherlock Holmes would have done.

But she also had to be careful and not let anyone guess that she knew. So she tidied her dress, wiped cobwebs off her face, and walked into the kitchen looking as prim and innocent as she could.

Luncheon was a hot meal of gravy and dumplings. Alys, the cook, was serving it. She was a short and plump woman with glossy black hair like a doll's. She stared at Seren curiously and bobbed a curtsy. "*Bore da*, miss."

Seren stared. "Hello. Is that Welsh? I don't know any Welsh."

"Ah, but you do, lovely!" Alys carried the hot plate to the table in a cloth and uncovered it carefully. "Because your very own name is Welsh, isn't it?"

"Is it?"

"You don't know that *seren* means star? How could you not know that, lovely?"

Star! Seren liked that. But she didn't waste time talking; instead, she ate quickly. It was a habit left over from her years at St. Mary's, because there, if you didn't gobble it down at once, the bigger girls took your food. She knew why no one had ever told her about her name; no one at St. Mary's would have even known where Wales was.

As she licked the last morsel of meaty gravy from her fork, she frowned. She had never had a home, not really, all her life. Maybe Wales was her home.

But you couldn't have a home without a family, and there was none here.

Just then a boy with black hair and a rough gray coat came in and spoke to the cook; he was given a plate and a glass of ale and he carried them out. Clods of mud slid from his boots.

Mrs. Villiers shook her head at him in annoyance.

"Wipe your boots next time, boy, or you'll get no dinner."

As he went, he glanced at Seren, curious and quick.

He must be the boy who did the garden.

Gwyn.

By three o'clock, Seren was bored and lonely, lying on her bed. There was no one to talk to. She was desperate to find out more about the locked room, but Mrs. Villiers had ordered her to her bedroom to rest. She didn't need rest. She had been trying to read, but her favorite books—even Mr. Sherlock Holmes himself—couldn't hold her attention.

If only she could be like him, brilliant and energetic! She would solve the mystery of the locked attic, and everyone would be amazed, and there would be a celebration and a Christmas tree!

Outside the window, it was already getting dark. Only the faint outline of the moon hung over the dark wood.

She lay on her bed and stared up at the ceiling. Surely there was something she could do. Draw a picture? Write a story? Sew that button on her gray chemise?

Instead, she rolled over and looked at the newspaper parcel.

It lay on the table as if it were waiting for her. That was a silly idea, but suddenly all she wanted to do was put the clockwork crow together and see what it looked like. There would be no harm in it; if the thin stranger turned up, she could always take it apart again.

She slid down and went to the table. There was a stump of yellow candle in the holder. She lit it from the fire, and it threw fluttering shadows around the room. She pulled up a chair. The moon was shining in now, and on the paper she read the words again. *For the journey is long and the road leads into darkness.*

For a moment, a shiver went down her spine.

Don't be silly, she told herself firmly. *It's only a toy.*

She tipped all the pieces out.

It took a while to figure out how to put it together. It was like a jigsaw puzzle—you had to work out which piece fit where—but it was more interesting. There were small cogs that clicked into each other, tiny wheels that screwed in. If you turned one, it moved with soft, whispery clicks. She arranged all the pieces in order, small right up to big, and tried each cog and wheel in turn. Gradually, as the hours passed and the moon climbed in the window and the candle guttered, the clockwork bird came together.

When she finally paused and sat back, she saw that she had assembled a small metal skeleton. She slipped it inside the feathered body and fastened some small buttons. Two wings fit into slits in the side. A pair of thin legs, made from wire, had to be pushed in, too, and their talons carefully unfolded. The head screwed on, a bit rustily, and then she added the beak, though it was hard to get that to fit straight. It ended up with a wry twist that she couldn't get rid of.

The Crow stood on the table. All that was needed now were its eyes. Bright as diamonds, they glinted wickedly in the firelight.

She clicked one in, and then the other.

The Clockwork Crow was complete.

Seren sat back, a little disappointed. After all that work, it was an awkward, clumsy-looking thing. Some of the feathers were moth-eaten, and they were missing in places on one wing. It looked like someone's old toy.

Rubbish, really.

There was a small, square keyhole in the side. She

might as well wind it up and see if it worked, so she rummaged around for the key and found it at the bottom of the newspaper, red with rust. She rubbed the rust away and fit it into the lock.

At that moment, there was a soft tap on her door.

Seren almost jumped. She said, "Hello? Who's there?"

No one answered. There was a sort of slithering shuffle outside. Then another noise, as light as if small nails had scratched it.

The cat!

She put the key down and hurried across, pulling the door open. "Come on, then, I can hear you . . ."

There was no cat there.

Surprised, she poked her head out and looked up and down the corridor. It was empty, the moonlight slanting through a window at the far end.

Strange. She had heard it, hadn't she?

Then, as she stepped back, she saw something on the floorboard by her foot, something wet and silvery. She knelt and touched it, and her hand jerked back with the shock.

It was ice.

A little pool of melting ice.

SHE ASKS A QUESTION

Where's the princess? Where's the boy?
Where the singing? Where the joy?

I f only," Mrs. Villiers muttered as the coach rattled down the lane, "we could have gotten some new clothes made in time. That coat is an absolute disgrace."

Seren frowned. "You brushed it."

"That did little to help. Besides, it's far too small for you. Tomorrow afternoon, we will have the dressmaker from the village in and begin at once. You are Captain Jones's goddaughter and you must look the part." She put her pale purple gloves together and held her small bag tight on her lap.

Seren shrugged and stared out at the passing countryside. How could you be someone's goddaughter if you'd never even seen them?

But new clothes would be nice, anyway.

They were going to church. Already, she could see the small gray building with its squat tower up on the hillside, half hidden by trees, and behind it the misty outlines of great mountains with rain clouds in their hollows.

The coach pulled up. Denzil opened the door and unfolded the step. Mrs. Villiers said, "I hope I can trust you to behave, Seren?"

"I've been to church before, Ma'am."

The housekeeper looked at her in distaste. "You are such an impudent girl."

Was she? As they got out and walked up the path between the gray, leaning graves, Seren wondered, because she just felt normal. And a bit tired. It had been hard to go to sleep last night. Twice she had jumped up in bed, wide awake, afraid she had heard that shuffling tap again, and twice she had tiptoed to the door and opened it, almost too scared to peek out.

There had been nothing there.

But what if Tomos was being kept a prisoner in the attic? What if he was being held for ransom or had become dangerous, and what if he came out at night and crept around?

She would feel much safer if there was some way of locking her bedroom. But there was no key, and she didn't dare ask for one. Mrs. Villiers certainly would want to know why.

The church was small and had that earthy smell she knew from the orphanage chapel. It was bitterly cold. The wooden pews were full of people, and as Mrs. Villiers swept up the aisle with Seren's hand in hers, all of them turned to stare.

For a moment, Seren felt small and self-conscious. Then she lifted her chin and tried to look haughty and important. After all, she was from the big house now.

With a shuffling of feet, the first hymn began, then the prayers, all in Welsh. Seren sat through the service in a daydream, her eyes exploring every corner, the angels in the ceiling, and the dingy stained glass. She watched the bobbing of the lady organist's hat, and saw the moment when the vicar tripped on the hem of his robe and stumbled on the pulpit step.

She smiled a secret smile.

There were tombs in here, too. From her seat, she could see at least six, and they were all of the Jones family—one of them really old, with a man and woman in ruffs and doublets lying down, a small line of their children kneeling around them.

She began to think about Tomos. Why would no one tell her anything about him? She should ask questions, investigate.

She nodded, her hands folded tight together in her gloves. She would look into the case.

"*You know my methods, Watson,*" she breathed.

Mrs. Villiers gave her a sideways glare.

After the service, the vicar shook everyone's hand and Mrs. Villiers chatted with people. Seren hung about by the church gate, awkward, because women were looking at her and it was embarrassing. One said, "Poor orphan lamb," and another, "Hello, *cariad.*"

"Hello," she muttered.

Mrs. Villiers was talking to the vicar. ". . . quite a responsibility, and of course, no help at all from the family. One shouldn't be surprised, in the circumstances."

He nodded sadly. "Of course, with the terrible mystery of—"

Mrs. Villiers interrupted him hastily. "Yes . . . Indeed."

"They're all gossiping about you," a voice said behind Seren.

She turned, expecting Denzil, but instead it was a boy. He was a bit taller than her, and his hair was dark and spiky. He was the boy she had seen in the kitchen yesterday.

He was in his Sunday suit now, washed and brushed. But there was still a bit of mud on his ear.

"I'm Gwyn."

"Hello. I'm Seren."

"You're not. You're *Miss* Seren."

She was surprised. "Am I? Does that mean I'm not supposed to speak to you?"

He laughed, but it wasn't a real laugh. "Yes, it does. I'm just the stable lad. Denzil would clip my ear if he saw us."

Seren shrugged. "I like Denzil."

"He's all right. What do you think about Mrs. V?"

Seren rolled her eyes. "I don't know. It's like she's annoyed with me all the time. Just for being me."

The boy frowned. "You'll get used to her."

They were silent a moment, watching the people

chat among the graves. It was so cold that Seren jumped on and off the small curb, trying to keep warm.

Gwyn looked at the sky. "There's bitter weather coming. Tonight or tomorrow."

"Is there? That's great!"

"For you, it might be. Not for me, with the horses to take out."

She stopped and stood still. "Gwyn, can I ask you a question?"

"What?"

"Do you know where Tomos is?"

He stared at her in sudden alarm. Then he stepped back quickly. "I'm not allowed to talk about that."

"Why not? No one talks about him. It's as if there's some mystery . . ."

"*They*'ve got him. The Family. That's what I think."

Seren's heart thumped with excitement. "What do you mean, got him?"

He looked around as if to be sure no one was near. Then he whispered, "I can't tell you. It's a secret. But . . . well, I think Tomos is being kept prisoner by—"

"*Hey!* You, boy! Come and hold the heads of those horses before they stamp this wall away!" Denzil had come up behind them, and his face was red with cold and anger.

Gwyn touched his cap and ran, with one warning glance at Seren.

Denzil watched him go. "You, miss, should not be chatting with stable boys." The small man gave her a hard glare. "What nonsense was he telling you?"

"Nothing. And I'll chat with who I want."

"You're a cheeky little madam." But he wasn't angry with her. Suddenly he seemed tired and sad, his hair a thick thatch of black. He said, "Come on. Time we got you back."

He took her elbow and almost pushed her up the step into the carriage. Seren was furious. She stared out of the window, and when Mrs. Villiers climbed in, she refused to say a word all the way until they reached the house. Then she ran upstairs, pulled off her bonnet and coat, and flung them in a heap on the bed.

Who did Denzil think he was! Why were they trying to keep her on her own all the time?

What was going on here?

Her room was cold. The fire had gone out. Sunday lunch would not be ready for an hour. She pulled a blanket off the bed, tugged it around her, and tried to calm down. What had that boy meant? That Tomos was a prisoner? Where? Who was keeping him locked up and why would they do that?

Then she heard a creak outside. She hurried over to her door and opened it. She crept to the end of the corridor.

Mrs. Villiers was coming upstairs. She was carrying a small tray, and it looked like there was a plate of food and a cup on it.

Seren's eyes widened. Who was that for? Quickly, she ducked behind a curtain.

Mrs. Villiers came up and went to the bottom of the attic stairs. She stopped and looked around, a sharp sideways glance. Then she climbed the white stairs.

Seren shrank into the shadows. She tiptoed back to her room and closed the door without a sound.

Mrs. Villiers was taking food to the attic! So that meant there had to be someone up there. Who else could it be but Tomos?

She was so excited she couldn't breathe and had to lean against the table.

If only she could get into the attic. She would have

·*★·➴*·· 60 ··*·◡·.*★

to spy and prowl and watch and find a way. Maybe . . .

Then she stopped in surprise.

The Clockwork Crow was lying on its side.

How had that happened? Surely she had left it standing upright on its weak wire legs?

One of its small, bright eyes was looking straight at her.

She remembered how she had been interrupted last night, so now she picked up the key, pushed it into the hole in the side of the bird, and wound it.

The machinery grated, stiff and rusty. It was hard to get the key around more than a few turns. There was a loud *whirr* and clatter. Quite suddenly, the Crow's head lifted. Its wings twitched in a scatter of dust. It took a single wobbly step.

Hardly worth all the hard work, she thought.

But then the Crow looked at her with its shiny eye and opened its twisted beak.

"Oil!" it croaked. "I need oil."

Seren blinked. She stared at it, astonished. "What?"

"Oil. Are you listening?"

She couldn't believe this. What sort of toy answered questions?

The Crow creaked its head painfully and stared around the room. "What a dump! Obviously I'm not in some palace. And it's freezing cold in here."

Seren was silent with amazement. The bird tried to extend a wing and flap it but made only a horrible rusty noise. "I'm so stiff! How long have I been in pieces?"

She had no idea. "You . . . you're talking to me."

The Crow made a scornful croak that might have been a laugh. "Clever, aren't we? Yes, I'm talking to you. Why shouldn't I talk to you? *Kek kek*."

"There's no need to be sarcastic."

"Who's sarcastic? Just get me some oil, stupid girl, because otherwise . . ." Its bright eyes widened in anger. "No! Not yet . . . wait a bit . . ."

Its voice slowed down, whirring to a juddering halt.

"Get . . . me . . . some . . . oi . . ."

Then it was still, frozen with one wing out and its head twisted awkwardly.

Seren came close and touched it. It felt cold and hard. Cogs and wheels churned to a slow silence inside it.

"That. Is. Amazing," she whispered.

She ate her lunch at such a speed, Mrs. Villiers scolded her twice. "For heaven's sake, Seren, your manners are appalling. Please take your elbows off the table, and don't shove the peas into your mouth like that. What's more, this morning at church, you were quite clearly not paying attention to the sermon. You're not paying attention now. *Seren!*"

She jumped. "What? Sorry."

"This won't do at all." Mrs. Villiers rang the bell. Because it was Sunday, they were having the meal in the housekeeper's room, a cozy parlor with a warm fire. Her face was red with the heat. "You need strict attention. I will write to Lady Mair. You must have some sort of governess. I can't be expected to do everything. I have enough to do."

A governess! Seren wasn't sure she liked the sound of that. Being supervised all the time would be like being back at St. Mary's, and already she had begun to enjoy the freedom of Plas-y-Fran.

"I'm sorry," she said hastily. "I'll try harder. Honestly. Look." She sat up and folded her hands neatly together.

Alys came in and cleared the plates. "Pardon me, Ma'am, but the mail has come. Will you sort it, or . . ."

"I'll see to it." Mrs. Villiers rose and went out, and the cook followed. Immediately Seren jumped from her chair and ran to the sideboard. It was full of small brown drawers marked with old-fashioned labels. BARLEY SUGAR, COCOA AND CHOCOLATE, ALL SORTS OF SEEDS, ISINGLASS SHAVINGS, HEARTSEASE. She pulled them open hastily. They contained spicy mixtures smelling sharp and pungent, but none of them were what she wanted. Then, on a shelf, she saw a small flask labeled OIL OF CLOVES.

She snatched it down, thrust it in her pocket, and was back in her chair as Mrs. Villiers came in, sorting through the letters.

"Ah, yes . . . Here's one from Lady Mair. Now we'll see."

The housekeeper opened it and read it quickly, her eyes scanning the lines, her mouth pursed up tight. "She says she hopes you are settling in and are happy here."

"Very," Seren said quietly.

"And that you are no trouble to Denzil and myself."

Seren chewed her lip. "I won't be."

Mrs. Villiers sniffed. "She encloses a money order for me to buy you a new coat and dresses. I hope you realize, Seren, how very, very lucky you are."

"I do, Mrs. Villiers. I really do."

Mrs. Villiers threw her a suspicious glance. "Good. Now go to your room and rest. Read only your Bible, make no noise, and do not leave the house. This is the Day of the Lord and we must be respectful."

Seren walked sedately out, straight-backed, past Denzil, who stared at her in surprise. She tripped up the stairs, only one at a time, then walked along the corridors and passageways, but as soon as she was sure no one could hear her, she ran, racing over creaky floorboards to her room, where she shut the door tight and even jammed a small stool in front in case anyone tried to come in.

The Crow stood on the table, a frozen bird.

She pulled out the oil.

"I've brought it!" she whispered.

THE ENCHANTED PRINCE

Beak and wing and eye and claw.
I'm not who I was before.

After a lot of rubbing with the oil, the key was shiny. It turned more easily. At once, the bird gave a groan and moved its wing feebly.

"I'm in agony here! Hurry up, girl. Hurry."

She dropped spots of oil on its neck, in the feathers of its wings, on its talons. The bird flexed and slid with little scratches against the table.

"Oh yes. That is so good! A bit more there . . . and yes, just there. At last!" It had both its wings spread out now. Before Seren could step back, it flapped them and, with a sudden lurch, it was flying, soaring wildly around the ceiling, almost crashing into the mirror.

Seren ducked. "Hey! Be careful!"

The Crow smacked into the curtains and got tangled. Its voice came out muffled. "Who put these here?"

"Let me help."

"No!" Its head appeared, then its body, and it was off again, zigzagging from the wardrobe to the canopy, from the dressing table to the window seat. It went so fast and looked so out of control, she was afraid it would smash into the glass, but then it was really looping around and around the room and making a sort of creaky, triumphant laugh.

Seren grinned, sitting cross-legged on the bed, and watched.

Finally, the Crow crash-landed on the table, skidded across the polished wood, and fell off into a basket of coals by the fire.

It swore, climbed out, and walked across the table, leaving sooty footprints.

"I needed that," it said.

"Are you all right?"

The Crow looked down its beak at her. "Why shouldn't I be? I'm just out of practice. So. Who are you and where is this pit of a house?"

It's so rude! she thought. But she said, "I'm Seren Rhys. This is a house called Plas-y-Fran. It's in Wales."

"Wales! How did I get here?"

"I brought you. Well . . . it was a sort of accident, really. You were in pieces in a newspaper parcel and . . ."

The Crow shuddered. "A newspaper parcel! How incredibly humiliating. How dare you wrap me in some dirty old newspaper!"

"I didn't."

"You just said . . ."

"No, it wasn't me, it . . ."

The Crow held up one wing. "Forget it. You're obviously confused. So then, you're a princess?"

Seren laughed. "No!"

"A duchess?" The Crow tipped its head. It seemed dismayed. "A marquise, a contessa? A baroness at least?"

She shrugged. "None of them. I'm an orphan. I've only just come here, mostly because the family feels sorry for me, I suppose. Not that I've even met any of them yet."

The Crow's beak opened in astonishment. It looked devastated. "An orphan! This is ridiculous! How can I possibly be expected to be unspelled in a place like this?" Then, as if it had a sudden idea, it hopped closer and looked hard at her. "Of course, you might actually be a princess in disguise. You were probably abandoned in a cradle on the river. Or left in the woods by your wicked stepmother."

"That just happens in stories." Seren knelt on the bed and inched a bit closer. "Are you . . . real?"

"As real as you," the Crow snapped.

"I mean alive."

"So do I. Do I look dead?" The Crow was disgusted. It stared out at the moon with its jewel-bright eyes. "This is what always happens. The clockwork runs out and no one winds me up. I'm sick of it. Whole centuries go by and I have no idea what's going on. Then I wake up in some rubbish house with some infant child." It turned its head, sly and sidelong. "So if it wasn't you, who put me in the parcel?"

"A thin man. He was so scared!"

"A thin man! Very tall?"

"Yes! Do you know him?"

"I might . . . Scared of what?"

"*Them.*"

The Crow looked thoughtful. "Them?"

"That's all he said. He went out and never came back, and I brought it . . . I mean, you . . . here and put it . . . I mean, you . . . together." An idea was coming to her, from all the fairy stories she had ever read. "Are you really under a spell?"

The Crow nodded sarcastically. "Clever girl. Worked it out all by yourself?"

"Are you a prince?"

The Crow blinked. Then it said, "What else? Prince of Siberia, and Trebizond, and the Glass Isle of Avalon."

She had never heard of any of those places and was not sure they even existed, but it wouldn't hurt to get off the bed and bob a curtsy, so she did. The Crow seemed pleased.

"Thank you," it said. "*Kek kek.*"

"So, that means you can do things? Magic and stuff?"

It looked smug. "A few tricks. A trifling set of sorceries."

"Can you open a locked room?"

The Crow looked at her with scorn. "That's child's play."

She wanted to race up to the attic at once, but first there was Sunday supper.

"Look, I have to go back downstairs for a bit. I won't be long, I promise. Will you be all right here? Do you need food or anything?"

"Food! This accursed spell means I can't eat or drink. For a hundred years I've dreamed of cheese and chocolate . . . truffles and toast . . ." It was gazing into the fire with a wistful look. But then it turned its jewel-bright eyes on her. "Wait a minute! I haven't given you permission to go anywhere."

Seren snorted. "I'm not your servant."

"That's what you think," the Crow said darkly. "Well, this time I'll allow it. But don't tell anyone about me."

"As if I would!"

It flapped to the window and stared out moodily. "And be quick! I get bored easily."

Supper was in the kitchen. Seren was so excited at the thought of the Crow, she hardly knew what she was eating or drinking. An enchanted prince! This was wild! And what did it mean by sorceries? What sort of things could it do?

Alys had been allowed to sit with them and, when Mrs. Villiers was busy making more tea, she whispered, "You're miles away, lovely."

"Just thinking." Seren spooned marmalade on her toast. Then she said, "Do you make all the food, Alys?"

"Don't I just! Baking, brewing, dairying, I have to do everything these days! Before last year, there were twenty servants in the house and more in the garden. It was all so much better then, before . . ." Then she stopped.

Seren swallowed a mouthful of toast. "Before what?"

Alys sighed and looked over slyly at Mrs. Villiers. "I can't say, lovely."

"Was it something to do with Tomos?"

The cook's red knuckles went tight on her teacup. "Whatever makes you think that?"

"I know it was," Seren said quietly. "I know there's a secret about him."

Alys stared at her. "Do you?"

"I know more than you think."

The cook's eyes were wide and startled, but Mrs. Villiers was near now, scolding the cat for being under her feet, and there was no time to say anything more.

After supper, Mrs. Villiers lit a candle for Seren from the one on the mantelpiece. "Time for bed." Outside, the wind was gusting; it rattled against the windows and the door shuddered, as if someone had tried the handle.

"Listen to it," Alys said. She seemed nervous. "I hate these wild nights."

"Where's Denzil?" Seren asked.

Mrs. Villiers looked sour. "Sunday evening is Denzil's night visiting his old mother. He'll not be home before midnight."

As she stood up, Seren wondered if they were scared of being alone in the big empty house. Because she had the sudden sense that the two women were listening, as if the roar of the rising storm out there in the trees and over the lake was a threat.

Mrs. Villiers turned abruptly. "Bed. Right now."

Seren hurried out, along the passageways and up the vast stairs. The candle threw her shadow wide and high. Small drafts lifted the edges of curtains and stirred tiny whirls of dust on the floorboards.

There was a strange feeling about this house. A secret sadness. As if everyone in it was afraid.

Back in her room, she looked around for the Crow, but it was nowhere to be seen.

A stab of dismay went right through her. Had it gotten out somehow? Had it flown away?

"Where are you?" she whispered.

"In here." The bird slid out from the wardrobe and flapped creakily up to the curtain rail. "I thought you might be the housemaid."

"They haven't got any housemaids."

"Good grief." The Crow shook its head in disbelief.

"Well, they used to, but . . ." She sat at the table and told the Crow all about Sir Arthur and Lady Mair going away, and the mysterious silence about Tomos. "No one will even talk about him. But I'm sure—almost sure—that there's someone locked up in that attic room. And who else could it be?"

The Crow scratched its head. "That's the door you want me to open?"

"Yes. And I want you to do it now, because they'll all have gone to bed."

"It's ridiculous. Why would they lock him up?"

She shrugged. "I don't know!"

"You read too much rubbish." The Crow made a

creaky wave of its wing. "I've been looking at your books. Sherlock Holmes! You should read more challenging things. French and math and chemistry. Some history—the Romans and Celts. Bible study, of course . . . What on earth is your governess thinking of?"

Seren scowled but tried to stay calm. She needed this infuriating creature. She said, "I haven't got a governess. And I don't really think you can do it."

"Do what?"

"Open the door."

"Of course I can!"

She stood up. "Come on, then, show me. Before Denzil gets back."

She took the candle with her but sheltered the flame with her hand as she ran up the attic stairs, because the draft was guttering it. The Crow flew overhead, a dark shadow under the ceiling. Once, it nearly hit a beam and had to swerve.

"Be careful!" Seren gasped.

"I told you, I'm just out of practice." Furious, it perched on a shelf and flicked dust from its feathers.

"This place is filthy. I really think you could have brought me somewhere better than this."

"I didn't want to bring you!"

"Well, you should have left me. Even a railway station waiting room would have been an improvement."

It made her angry. "You're so ungrateful. After I put you together and oiled you!"

The Crow snorted. "It wasn't even proper oil. I stink like a spice rack!"

She didn't trust herself to speak. She marched down the corridor. Then, as she got closer to the locked door, she slowed and stopped. "This is it."

The Crow swooped up beside her and perched on the handle. It seemed to swell up with self-importance. Its head tipped sideways to the keyhole. "Can't hear anything."

Neither could she. The room beyond the locked door was silent.

"But I'm sure, before, I heard breathing."

"Breathing! Nonsense!"

Seren ignored it. She tapped softly on the white wood.

"Hello? Is anyone there? Tomos? It's me, Seren."

The Crow snorted. "There's no one there."

"There is."

"There's not."

"Can't you just open it?"

"That won't take magic." It flew suddenly up to the top of the doorframe, picked up something in its beak, and dropped it at her feet. "Just use that."

Seren jumped. A large key had landed on the floor with a loud bang. "What is wrong with you? You'll wake everyone up!"

"Not my problem." The Crow looked down its beak at her. "Well. If you're so brave, open it."

Her heart was thumping. She bent and picked up the key.

Carefully, quietly, she threaded it into the lock and creaked open the door.

Then she peered inside.

GLASS AND SNOWFLAKES

In the silent night,
Secret creatures wait.

I t *was* a nursery.

That was clear at once, even though the room was dark. The candle flame glimmered on mirrors and glassy surfaces. As Seren crept in, she caught reflections of herself everywhere.

"Hello?" she whispered. "Tomos?"

"You really don't give up, do you?" The Crow had flitted in behind her and was perched on the top of the soldiers' fort. "There's no one here but us, girl. And if you ask me, there hasn't been for ages."

She had to agree. The table and chairs were covered with white sheets. The floor was so dusty, her footprints were clear. As she reached out and touched the rocking horse, it moved with a soft creak, as if it hadn't been used for some time.

"And that," the Crow remarked acidly, "is the breathing noise you heard. Just a creaky old toy."

"The same as you, then," Seren snapped. She was so disappointed. She hadn't realized until now how much she wanted Tomos to be here, to have someone to be friends with in this dark, sad house. She closed the door and stood with her back against it. Mysterious shapes glittered on all the tables and shelves; small, glinting objects. What were they?

"Light the lamp," the Crow commanded.

There was an oil lamp on the table with a little fuel left. Seren turned the wick up and lit it from the candle, then put the glass cover on. As the yellow light grew, she turned around.

And gasped.

The room was full of glass globes.

A whole collection of them lined every shelf. She picked up the nearest; it was heavy. Inside it was a Father Christmas on his sleigh outside a house just like Plas-y-Fran, with a silver paper lake and tiny trees made of pipe cleaner.

"Snow globes!"

She put it down and shook another, and a paper snowstorm swirled over a tiny church with metal foil windows. "Look at them all!" Some were as large as fishbowls, others tiny. Seren went around shaking them one after another, creating a whole room of secret snowstorms. She laughed, astonished.

Then she saw the smallest one. It was on the table next to the bed.

It was different from the others, the glass greener and thicker, and somehow what was inside it seemed more real. She picked it up. She saw a white palace, all turrets and pinnacles, and when she shook the globe, the snow inside was soft and strange. It fell like real snow fell, and for a moment, it made her heart turn cold.

The Crow was striding among the globes, staring in at itself. Its beak and jewel-bright eyes shone in a hundred reflections. "This is a bit weird, really. I mean, why not collect something better, like diamonds or sapphires, something worth money?"

"Maybe he just liked them. He's only a boy."

The Crow made a harsh croak. "Boys! I know all about boys! It's still odd."

She had to admit it puzzled her, as well. Boys collected stamps or coins or conkers or, well, boyish things. Glass globes of falling snow did seem a strange hobby. But there were other toys in here, too, and she could see them clearly now: a fort with toy soldiers all lined up and tiny cannons to fire; a bow and arrows; many books; and a great heap of building blocks stacked into a half-built castle. There was a box of paints left open so they had dried up, and a brush in a jam jar where the water had all evaporated. A sketchbook lay open; she picked it up and saw a drawing of a forest, the trees all made of silver and gold, with small lanterns hanging in the branches. It was a mysterious painting. Much better than she could ever do. It was signed *Tomos Jones*.

She shook her head. "It's like . . . like he just left everything. Just went out and never came back. It doesn't make sense."

"He's probably with his mother." The Crow was too interested in trying to peck a shiny silver coin out of a can to pay attention.

"No. If he's in London, why are his toys all here? His clothes in the wardrobe, his shoes under the bed? Why is the place all locked, and above all, why . . ."

The Crow's head snapped up. "Shh!"

"Stop telling me what to do!"

"Shut up!" Its hiss was urgent. "I can hear someone!"

Seren froze. They listened, intent. Then yes, she could hear it, a soft footstep far below!

"Out! Now!" Seren took one step, then whirled back and snuffed the lamp. A smell of warm wick hung in the room.

"They'll smell it," the Crow remarked.

"Can't help that. Hurry!"

"Worried, aren't we?" the Crow said, maddeningly calm. "But what if they find you? What can they do?"

"I don't want to be found! And you might get taken apart again and end up back in the newspaper."

The Crow's calmness changed instantly to horror. "Let's go!"

She still had the strange, small snow globe in her hand, but as she darted to the door, she dropped it and it rolled under the bed.

"Leave it!" the Crow hissed.

But she couldn't; there was something magical about it, so she scrabbled hurriedly under the bed after it. The dark space was filthy with dust; she had to stretch her arm right out, groping to find the glass globe. Then her fingers touched something small but square. It felt like a tiny book. It had been jammed under the springs of the bed, in a secret place.

"Come on!"

Seren tugged the book down, grabbed the snow globe, and squirmed out, sneezing from the dust. The book was purple, with the word DIARY written carefully on its cover. Small snowflakes had been drawn all over it.

"Look at this!"

"No way. I'm off!" The Crow shot out, a shadow into the darkness. Seren slid after it, locked the door, and looked around swiftly for something to stand on, because there was no other way she could reach to put the key back up on the lintel. But there was nothing, and the footsteps were coming closer up the stairs.

"Crow!"

No answer.

Seren ground her teeth. She dropped the key on the floor and ran.

She just made it to an alcove before Denzil turned the corner of the corridor. Flattened behind a hanging curtain, she held her breath as he walked past her. He carried a lantern and he was checking all the windows; his shadow moved above him on the ceiling.

The curtain was so dusty, she wanted to sneeze again. She crammed both hands over her face and shuddered out a silent explosion. When she dared peek out, she saw he had come to the nursery door.

He tried the handle.

Then, as he turned away, he stopped, and she knew he had seen the key because the lamplight distorted, as if he had bent to pick it up.

Seren put her eye closer to a tiny gap in the curtain.

The small man was looking at the key. He gazed sharply up the empty corridor; she kept still, terrified he would see her.

He slipped the key into his pocket and came back, this time passing so close that his sleeve brushed against her hiding place.

The light faded.

He went softly down the stairs, and then it was dark.

Seren waited at least five minutes until the house was completely silent before she moved. Her candle had been left in the nursery, so she had to feel her way down the stairs a step at a time until her hand touched the smooth wooden ball at the bottom of the banister.

Moonlight slanted through the gaps in the shutters, all down the creaky corridor.

She slipped silently along to her bedroom, opened the door, and whisked in. As she did so, a shadow detached from a high picture frame and slid in beside her.

Seren crumpled on the floor, breathless. "That was so close!"

"Did he know you were there?"

"He found the key, but he didn't go in." She could only see the Crow's eyes, glittering in the moonlight. "If he does, he'll find the candle. They'll know it was me."

"Of course. Serves you right for being so careless . . ."

"Do you think they'll lock me up, too?"

The Crow croaked in scorn. "*Kek kek*. No one's locked up. The boy wasn't there, was he? You've got him on the brain. Now I'm exhausted. I'm going to have a well-deserved rest. Don't wake me." It flapped into the wardrobe, put its head under its wing, and was silent.

Seren undressed and climbed into bed, but it was a long time before she could even think about sleeping. The moon was shining in on her, and her heart was still beating fast with excitement.

Where was Tomos?

Why was his room abandoned?

And what was in the diary she had pushed so carefully under her pillow?

Her hand, in the darkness, smoothed its velvet cover. It must hold so many secrets. She couldn't wait to read it.

Then she sat up and listened. Outside her window, the softest of hisses made her pad over and pull back the corner of the curtain. She gasped in delight.

It was snowing!

Flakes fell and swirled in a silent dance. Just like in the snow globe she had shaken. As if she had made the snow come. By magic!

By morning, the watery sun was back, but the lawns and trees were white and smooth. At breakfast, everyone seemed excited. Denzil brought a great load of logs in and muttered, "Glorious out there!" Slush slid off his boots. But Mrs. Villiers just frowned and said, "More mess for us to clean, that's all."

Seren looked up. "Can I go out in it? Please?"

Mrs. Villiers was silent. Then she said, "You may take a short walk."

Seren jumped down from the table. "Really?"

"But do *not* go through the iron gate."

"Oh . . ."

The housekeeper fixed her with a hard stare. "Are you questioning me?"

"No. Of course not." Seren backed toward the door.

"You will wear a coat, your boots, a scarf, a hat, and gloves."

But Seren was already thundering up the stairs. Bursting in, she gasped, "I'm going out in the snow!"

The Crow looked unimpressed. It was sitting by the small fire, hunched up. "Why would you want to? It's freezing enough in here."

She shrugged into her coat and grabbed some gloves. "Guard that diary. And the snow globe." She stopped dead. "Oh wait! Do you think they want me out of the way? To search my room?"

"For heaven's sake," the Crow muttered.

"Well, just make sure no one comes in."

The Crow threw her a withering look.

It was so good to go outside! She ran past the kitchen and found the servants' door, and then hurtled out into the white and silver world. The air was a shock of cold, the sky wide and purest blue. A thin layer of snow lay on every roof and window, and like lacework on the cobbled courtyard. She began to explore.

There were outbuildings and stables and carriage houses, a dairy and a laundry house, and they were all unused. Most of all, she wanted to find the gardens, and she came to them at last through an arch in an old brick wall. The flower beds were bare and frosted, the trees leafless. But the snowfall had turned everything white; every grass blade and crisp leaf was outlined in a fine fur of crystals. She took her gloves off and touched them; she ran over the grass and made crunchy footprints. Gates were frozen open, and everywhere birds were singing, as if they had to hurry because the hours of daylight were so few.

It was amazing! No Mrs. Villiers watching her every move, no Denzil lurking in dark stairways. After the sad and silent house, it made her feel alive. She ran so fast her breath came in gasps. She climbed down into the sunken garden and balanced along the low walls; she threw snowballs at trees and picked up dead leaves and conkers, hollow stems and holly berries.

It would be such a good idea to take armfuls of things in and make decorations for Christmas. There was ivy on all the walls, and mistletoe up in a high tree.

But Christmas preparations didn't seem to be happening at Plas-y-Fran. The whole thing would be miserable.

At the edge of the gardens was the shrubbery, and beyond that, a high brick wall. Seren ran alongside the wall, running her fingers over the frosty bricks, until she came to an iron gate. It was securely locked. This must be the way out to the park. Feeling like a prisoner, she gripped the bars and gazed through.

Wide lawns led down to the lake. It looked sinister against the whiteness of the grass, a murky expanse of dark water. There were no birds on it: no swans or ducks, which was strange. She wondered how deep it was. If only she could get through and run down there!

As she turned reluctantly away, she looked up at the house. Her own room was on the other side, but one of these windows must belong to the attic nursery. She tried to work out which.

Maybe that little one, high up, in a small gable of its own.

Then she gasped. Surely someone was standing behind the curtains of the room! A figure, dark in the shadows. Was it Tomos? Denzil?

She lifted her hand and waved. "Hey!" she yelled. "Hello!"

But maybe the figure stepped back, or the curtain drifted.

Because now the window was empty.

CAUGHT

Be careful going up the stair.
Someone's left their shadow there.

"Stand still. Or the pin will stick you."

"It just did!" Seren gasped as another pin jabbed her leg. "Ouch! Can't you be a bit more careful?"

Mrs. Villiers had pounced on her as she had trudged in, cold and puzzled, from the garden and brought her straight into the kitchen. A small fire made the room seem hot after being outside. "Dress off," Mrs. Villiers had ordered. Now Seren was standing on the table, and all around her was a swath of materials, dull blue cambric and boring gray wool. She was wearing one of the new dresses, and the seamstress, Mrs. Roberts, a small, neat woman who seemed too terrified of Mrs. Villiers even to speak, was pinning up the hem.

"It's too big," Seren objected.

"Of course it's big." Mrs. Villiers was watching. "You'll grow into it."

"I don't like the color. And it's scratchy."

Mrs. Villiers stood straight and unmoved by the fire. Her thin lips were set in a line. "You're an ungrateful girl."

"No, . . . I'm not. I'm the one who has to wear it, and I'm sure Lady Mair wouldn't want . . ."

"Don't you *dare* tell me what Lady Mair would want!" Mrs. Villiers's anger was so sudden and so explosive that Mrs. Roberts jumped in shock and Seren opened her eyes wide. "Lady Mair is the kindest lady and you have no idea—*no idea!*—of what she's been through! The heartbreak, the sheer anguish! No other family would have even considered taking in some orphan after what happened to . . ."

She stopped.

Everyone in the kitchen was breathless. Mrs. Roberts, with a mouthful of pins, seemed frozen in fear.

Mrs. Villiers turned and stormed out of the room, almost knocking over Gwyn, who was carrying in a box of stored apples.

Seren stared after her, amazed. What had brought that on? She hadn't meant to sound ungrateful. And surely those glints in the corner of Mrs. Villiers's sharp gray eyes couldn't have been tears, could they?

Gwyn unpacked the apples silently onto the table.

Mrs. Roberts carefully took the pins out of her mouth and whispered, "Better take the dress off now, dearie. I'll get the alterations done."

Seren climbed down from the table. "What did I say? I didn't mean anything . . ."

The seamstress shook her head and busied herself with packing up her things.

Seren looked at Gwyn. He frowned. Then he stepped closer and whispered, "It's not you. She thinks it was all her fault."

Seren frowned. "What was?"

But Mrs. Villiers was back, and if there had been any tears, they were gone now. Her face was white and her voice icy. "Get that dress off. And then go to your room."

﹏

"What does Mrs. Villiers think was her fault?" Seren sat on the window seat. "I don't get it. And if Tomos is not being kept in the attic, where is he? And why is everyone here so *scared*?"

The Crow, inspecting a moth hole in its wing, said, "Don't ask me. The whole place is dark and freezing. And look at me, I'm falling apart. If I was back in my palace now, it would be very different. I'd have a meal set before me, on gold and silver plates. I'd have musicians to play for me and dancers to dance. I'd have . . . er . . . well, other princely things. If I was human again."

Seren frowned. "So how does the spell get broken?"

"I don't know if it ever can be."

"Oh, come on!" She slid off and walked over to it. "They always can. In all the books I've read . . ."

"This is not in your silly books! This is real!" The Crow seemed nearly as cross as Mrs. Villiers. Seren sighed.

Trying to sound kind, she said, "You never explained to me how it happened."

"I don't want to talk about it."

"Suit yourself." She turned away, but the Crow said hastily, "But, of course, if you insist, I will. It's not a long story. One day I was out, er . . . hunting. Yes, hunting. Princes hunt all the time, don't they? I was riding through a dark wood and I met a witch."

"A witch?"

"She must have been a witch. She looked like a witch. With one of those crooked hats and a broomstick and everything. She was sitting by a well. She pointed a skinny finger at me. She said, 'Give me your jewels and your horse and your crown.' Well, of course I had no intention of doing any such thing, so I said, 'Don't be ridiculous. Get out of my way, please.' I was trying to be polite, but it was a mistake. She stood up and spoke one magic word, and I felt . . . well, it's hard to explain how weird it felt. I felt myself crumpling and crunching up. I felt my heart becoming a wheel and my bones becoming cogs and my muscles shrinking into springs. I fell off my horse. I tried to wave my arms, but all I had were wired wings. I tried to speak, but there was only a croak. Then she said, 'Until you give up the one thing that means the most to you, you'll be a black crow forever and ever.'"

Seren stared.

The Crow preened a feather flat. It looked rather smug.

"*The one thing that means the most? What's that?*"

"I have no idea."

She made a face. "It's a very strange story. I mean, to do that just because you . . ."

"Are you suggesting I've made it up?"

"No . . ."

"I am totally insulted!" The Crow shuffled around on the canopy and turned its back on her. "I'm not saying another word until you apologize. After all I've done for you!"

Seren sighed. "You haven't done anything for me." She was getting tired of everyone being cross with her. Instead of apologizing, she went downstairs and ate lunch so silently, Denzil observed her the whole time with his watchful eyes. Then, when she came back, she ignored the Crow, which was gazing at itself in the mirror. She got the diary out from its hiding place under her pillow and opened it. She lay on her stomach on the bed and began to read.

Tomos's diary was a real mess. His writing was a ragged scrawl; pictures and diagrams were everywhere, all over the pages. Nothing was in order. He seemed to be very interested in birds and animals; also there were a lot of drawings of battles and soldiers, and a whole section of notes about steam trains. Seren flipped through it with increasing disappointment. She had hoped for secrets, for strange messages asking for help, but this was just boy's stuff.

Then one sentence caught her eye.

Last night the bell rang again.

Seren sat up. The page was dated over a year ago.
"This could be interesting!"
"What?" the Crow muttered, preening a feather.
"Listen!" She began to read aloud.

It rang at midnight and woke me up. I had the candle all ready by my bed and was out in the corridor in a flash.

The moon was shining through the windows down the corridor.

I've worked out where the bell is ringing. It's deep under the house. So I ran down the stairs. The farther down I went, the more I felt the bell's shimmery echo. In places the walls looked like they were glittering with it, if a sound can glitter.

No one heard me. Mamma and Pa were in bed and all the servants must have been, too, although there was a lamp lit in the stable room where Denzil sleeps. An owl hooted—that brown one nesting in the clock tower.

The Crow cawed a harsh laugh. "Owls! They're such snobs."

"Shh!" She flipped the page. "He says he goes right down to the cellar. Then this."

Usually the cellar is dark and dusty but last night it was all different. There were some golden stairs that led downward. I've never seen them before. They went into the wall, but not into blackness; there was a sort of light, all silvery and shimmery, and it made patterns on my face.

I really wanted to go down.

But I knew if I did, it would be dangerous, because They were down there.

The Family.

I heard a sound. It was music, very soft, very quiet. It was coming up from far, far below.

I knew they wanted me to come. That there was a world down there, all shining and wonderful and full of magic. I put my hands over my ears, and I turned and ran, because otherwise they would have power over me. But it's too late. I can't get the sound out of my head. Such a sweet sound. I got into bed in all my clothes and my breathing was huge.

It's the most scared I've ever been.

I fell asleep after a while. But the weirdest thing was, today, when I went down to the cellar and looked, I knew what I would find.

No golden stairs. It was just all dark and dusty like it always is.

Seren looked up. "That is so strange! Who are the Family?"

The Crow shuffled on its perch. It looked at her sideways with its jewel-bright eye.

"Don't you know? The Fair Family. The Fae. You don't mess with Them."

"But I've heard that bell, too! It rang the first night I was here." Had she heard it since? She didn't think so. "So maybe he's locked in the attic to keep him from wandering back down there. Or . . ."

A loud knock rapped on the door. Seren was so startled, she dropped the diary. The Crow had barely time to freeze itself in an awkward pose before the door was flung open and Mrs. Villiers marched in. "Who were you talking to?"

Seren scrambled up, hands behind her back. "No one. Ma'am."

"I heard you, you were talking to someone."

"I was just . . . reading aloud."

Mrs. Villiers glared at her, then around at the bare room. She opened the wardrobe and ran her eye over the contents, then closed it with ominous quietness. "Your room needs to be kept tidier than this, Seren. We have no servants, remember. I expect you to dust it yourself and . . ." She stopped. "Goodness me. What on earth is that moth-eaten monstrosity?"

She had seen the Crow! She went right up to it.

Seren fidgeted in dismay. "That's . . . the toy. From the newspaper parcel."

"Good heavens." Mrs. Villiers circled the Crow, her arms folded, nose wrinkled in distaste. The Crow, standing as still as it could, stared past her with one glittering eye, but even so, Seren saw it wobble.

"That's the ugliest thing I've ever seen." Mrs. Villiers stretched out her hand. "It should go straight in the garbage."

"No!" Seren jumped forward. "No! You can't! It's mine!"

She had to do something before the Crow lost its temper and snapped out something. Before it pecked the woman's hand.

Mrs. Villiers looked furious. "You are the most impudent, forward little girl! I am not having such rubbish in the house. Get out of my way."

Seren stood firm. "I won't. It's mine and I want to keep it. You have no right to take my things!"

"You deserve a good slap."

"You wouldn't dare!"

"Indeed I would."

Face to face, they glared at each other.

"I'll write to Lady Mair," Seren hissed.

For a moment, the silence was terrible; then Mrs.

Villiers took a breath and stepped back. When she spoke, her voice dripped ice. "No, you won't. Because I will write to Lady Mair myself and advise that you should be taken back to the orphanage. This is quite clearly no place for you."

Seren was so shocked and angry the words burst out of her. "Why? Are you afraid I'll find out what you've done?"

"Done?"

"That you're keeping him prisoner?"

Mrs. Villiers stepped forward and grabbed her arm. "What are you talking about?"

Seren jerked away fiercely. "I'm talking about Tomos. I know you've had him hidden in that attic. And if you don't let me go, *right now*, I'm going straight to the police and I'm going to tell them."

Mrs. Villiers's face was as white as the wall. But she was not the one who answered. That was Denzil, standing breathless in the doorway as if all the shouting had brought him hurrying up.

"So now don't you think it's time to tell her?" he said. "About everything?"

LAST CHRISTMAS EVE

Footprints in the fallen snow.
Can you tell me where they go?

They had come down to the kitchen, where the cat lay curled on the hearth watching them in surprise.

Seren sat upright on the stool in the middle of the floor. She was still simmering with anger. If they sent her back to the orphanage, what did she care! It would be better than this cold, dark, empty place.

Mrs. Villiers swished past her and stoked the fire furiously. But it was Denzil who took charge. He stood in front of Seren, folded his arms, looked straight at her, and said, "So what's this silly idea you've got into your head about Tomos?"

"It's not silly. I saw you taking food up to him."

Denzil stared. "Up where?"

"The nursery. His room."

"Have you been in there?"

Seren looked up boldly. "Yes. I have."

"That is the absolute limit." Mrs. Villiers clasped her hands so tight, the fingers went white. "You broke in . . ."

"I didn't break in, I found the key. I didn't steal anything, and I don't think I even need to say sorry. Because I was just looking for Tomos. I thought I saw him in the window . . ."

"But you found the room dusty and empty," Denzil said.

She looked down, annoyed. "Yes."

The small man paced the floor. His voice was quiet and full of pain. "You've got everything wrong, girl. Mrs. Villiers was taking the food up to a workman who was here repairing a leak in the roof. It must have been him you saw. We've had a few drips coming through the ceiling. There was one right outside your bedroom door, didn't you notice? As for Master Tomos, he has not been in this house for a year. Yes, his clothes are here, his toys wait for him. But he's not here to play with them. He's not here to eat his bread and milk and entertain us all with his wild and funny tales. Master Tomos . . . is lost to us."

He looked so devastated, Seren felt shocked. And then, quite suddenly, she understood it all: their black clothes, the shuttered rooms, the absent parents, the sad, silent house.

"Oh," she said, putting her hands over her mouth. "Oh, Denzil, I'm so sorry! He's dead, isn't he? I'm so, so sorry . . ."

"Be quiet, Seren." Denzil's voice was harsh, but in a kindly way. He looked over at Mrs. Villiers. "You need to explain to her."

The housekeeper turned. Her face was white. "My orders were—"

"She needs to know. She'll be living here, and people talk, so she'll find out soon enough. Tell her now." He gathered up his coat and headed for the door. "I'll leave you to it."

He went out and the cat ran after him, leaving Mrs. Villiers in obvious dismay by the kitchen fire.

Slowly, she came and sat down, her back ramrod straight.

"How did it happen?" Seren didn't want to ask, but her imagination was racing, and for some reason she had to keep talking. "Was it the typhoid? At St. Mary's, a girl caught that and we all had to—"

"It wasn't typhoid."

"Did he drown? In the lake? It looks deep."

"Seren!" Mrs. Villiers held up a hand. "That's enough." She put both her hands in her lap and interlaced her fingers tightly. She looked most uncomfortable, as if she cursed Denzil for leaving this task to her. "Tomos is not dead. At least . . . we hope and pray that Tomos is not dead."

Seren stared. "You hope? You mean you don't know?"

"No, we don't know. Because Tomos is missing."

"Missing?"

"I'm afraid so." Her eyes were closed, and she looked older now. "Denzil is right; it will be easier to tell you. As you are clearly the sort who likes to pry into everything."

That was unfair. But Seren kept quiet. She wanted the story, and she was intensely interested.

"The facts are these. Tomos went out of the house for a walk after breakfast one morning, and he never came back."

Seren's eyes were wide. "When?"

"Last year. In fact, on Christmas Eve." Mrs. Villiers sat still, staring blankly across the room. "I will never forget that day. It had been snowing, and he had been clamoring to go and build a snowman, but Denzil was too busy decorating the hall to go with him. Captain Jones was working in the study upstairs. Lady Mair was in her sitting room, writing letters. Everyone was busy with the preparations for Christmas. I myself told him that he must stop bothering us and play on his own." She tensed her hands until the knuckles were white. "I wish . . . how I wish I had not said that."

For a moment, there was a flicker of something heartbroken in her eyes.

"So he put on his coat—he must have, because it was gone from the wardrobe—and let himself out of the house. There were other servants here then, and the captain's dogs; it was a busy, happy place, but no one saw him go. If only . . ." She shook her head. "If only someone had gone with him! But who would have guessed what would happen?"

"What did happen?" Seren asked, breathless.

"At lunchtime, we realized he had not come back. His

mother was cross, but no one feared anything. Denzil was sent out to find him; there were footprints in the snow, across the gardens and through the iron gate toward the lake, so he followed them. Tomos had run and played; there was a half-built snowman. And then . . ."

"Yes?"

"Then the footprints went on, down the snowy slope toward the lake. There's a deep hollow there, a sort of rocky grotto. The footprints climbed down into that place, among the brambles. And there they . . . ended."

"Ended?"

"Vanished."

"But that's not possible." Seren shook her head. "I mean, he must have gone somewhere."

"The footsteps stopped in the middle of a white snowfield. As if he had become invisible, or some flying creature had swept him away. Or as if the earth had opened and swallowed him." She smiled, and this time Seren saw there really were tears in her eyes. "That is fanciful nonsense, of course. It must have snowed again and covered his steps. He could not be found. Denzil came tearing back, poor soul. And soon Lady Mair was sobbing, in such fear."

Seren could imagine it, the house stirred up like a wasps' nest, everyone running everywhere, the servants' panic, the shouting of orders. It was like something in one of her books.

"For two days we searched. Dogs were used, but there was no scent. The local villagers came out, even in that bitter snow. There were tales of vagrants from the cities who kidnapped children for ransom. One of them had been seen here a few days earlier. Lady Mair lay in agony in her bed; I had to have the doctor give her sedatives or she would never have slept. The police of two counties were called out. But . . ."

"Nothing?"

"Nothing. Ever since that day. Nothing."

The cat came back and sat, looking up. Mrs. Villiers put down some scraps for it, and it ate them, its small red tongue working fast. Seren watched. What a story! No wonder the house was as sad as a graveyard. How they must have suffered, Lady Mair and Captain Jones! Had Tomos fallen into some cleft in the ground and died there of cold? Had he really been kidnapped?

"No one sent a ransom note? Asked for money?"

"No one." Mrs. Villiers's voice was harsh and stern.

She stood tall, and her face, though pale, was composed again, as if she had remembered that Seren was a stranger here. "Master Tomos has never been heard of again. It has devastated his parents. They cannot bear even to be near this house. The servants were sent away and only Denzil and I are left. So now you know the story."

"Yes, but—"

"No more will be said on the matter." Mrs. Villiers turned away. "I hope there will be no more nonsense about people being kept in attics. It would be better if you didn't go up to the nursery again. And . . ." She hesitated. "I may have been a little extreme in my anger earlier. But this is a house of sorrow, Seren, and we cannot have any more trouble here. So I warn you, overstep the mark once more and I will have you sent back to the orphanage. Do you understand?"

Seren nodded.

She left the kitchen and walked upstairs, the cat following her. Her mind was full of the story, and it was fascinating, though there was so much else she wanted to know.

People didn't just disappear.

She thought of the golden stairs Tomos had written about in the diary, the sweet, enticing music he had heard. And suddenly she knew who to ask.

All the next day, she hung around the house, keeping out of Mrs. Villiers's way. Then she wandered the gardens and looked in all the outbuildings, but it wasn't until late in the afternoon that she found Gwyn, out in the stable yard, piling hay with a pitchfork.

The sky was darkening over the trees on the hill.

He looked up when he heard her coming.

"I know about Tomos," she said quickly.

Gwyn stopped. He leaned on the fork. "Do you? Well, that's more than we do."

"I mean I know he's missing. And that you think he's been taken by the Family. But who are they?"

He shrugged. "The Tylwyth Teg. The Fair Family. Everyone knows that's what happens. They take children."

She shivered and came in and sat on a hay bale.

"We shouldn't talk about Them." He held up his fingers and they were crossed. "Don't ask me any more. They might hear." He glanced around, worried. "Especially when it's getting dark. You never know where They are, listening, watching you."

.·*. ✦ *·. III .·*. ✦ .*.

Seren was too curious to be afraid. "I don't understand. Are They human?"

"No. They are magic, secret creatures. They never get older, and They can be beautiful, or They can be ugly or twisted and wild. They live under the ground. Or maybe in the lake. This used to be all Their land, thousands of years ago, until people came. I think that's the reason. The Joneses took Their land. So They took the boy. My *nain* says it's happened before, over and over, with the children. They take them to a place where they never get older."

A sly whisper of wind made him stop. He started on the hay again, hastily. "Don't tell Denzil I told you. He knows, and Mrs. V, too, probably, but she won't admit it."

Seren shook her head. It sounded so strange, but she believed him. "So how can we get him back?"

"You can't. Not without magic and spells and all sorts of clever stuff. You don't know about any of that, do you?"

"No," she said. Then she smiled a small smile. "But I know someone who does."

Gwyn stared at her.

But she jumped up and ran back to the house.

"The Fair Family!" The Crow shook its head so hard, dust flew out. "No chance! Never in a million years. No way I would ever even consider it. They are the most dangerous and tricky of enemies to make. Good heavens! Witches are bad enough, but those creatures! If They've got Tomos, you can forget it. At least . . ."

"At least what?"

It was perched on the rim of the mirror. "Never mind. More important things. Did you get the ink?" It raised a wing and looked at its feathers critically in the glass. "She was quite right, that old nag of a house-keeper. I'm more than a bit moth-eaten. I've been shockingly neglected."

Seren sighed. She dipped the nib in the ink. "Keep still."

"It's not blue, is it?"

"It's black."

Carefully, she inked in one moth-eaten spot on the Crow's wing. The Crow giggled. "Ooh. That tickles."

She said quietly, "How do I rescue him?"

The Crow sighed. "Well, there is one way. You have to wait for a year and a day. Then the bell will ring, and the golden stairs will appear. That's your only chance."

"A year and a day. That's Christmas Day. Three days' time!"

"Just a little to the left." The Crow turned to show another moth hole. "But I'm not going down those stairs. The Fair Family are too dangerous. Besides, They want me."

Her hand paused in midair. "They want you?"

It puffed up its chest proudly. "Why do you think my . . . er . . . the man in the station was so scared? He knows They want me. They want to keep me in a cage of ice, and make me do tricks and magic for Them for all eternity, to amuse their king and queen and all Their horrible court. But if that happens, I'll never get unspelled. So if you go down there, you're on your own."

Seren scowled. "I rescued you. I put you together. And you are so ungrateful!"

She put the pen down. "Why am I doing this? I'm going to take you apart and put you back in the news-paper."

The Crow hopped away. "No, you're not!" It flew up

to the ceiling and perched on the very top of the canopy. "Try it and I'll fly out of the window. You'll never see me again."

"Oh yes?" Immediately she ran over, slammed the window shut, and locked it. Then she stopped, staring out through the glass. "Who's that?"

"Where?"

"Out there. At the edge of the lawn, just inside the wood. Someone's standing there, looking up at the house."

The Crow sidled nearer, curious. Then it stopped. "Oh no, you don't! That's just a trick to lure me down. You don't fool me." It turned its back, annoyed.

"No, there's really someone. It's a man." Seren tried to rub the frost off the window, but it was outside. She put her eye to the cold glass. Then she gasped and stepped back. "It's him!"

"Don't believe you. No one there."

"There is! It's the thin man from the railway station!"

The Crow turned its head. Curiosity was too strong, so it flew down and perched on her shoulder, digging its wiry talons into her skin.

"Ow!" she gasped.

"Keep still. Where? Ah, yes."

The thin man lurked in the shadow of the trees. He still had his midnight-dark coat on, and the hat was pulled even farther over his eyes. Seren thought he was probably shivering with cold. He was looking intently up at the windows. Then he ducked out of the trees and began to walk quickly toward the house.

The Crow gave a *kark* of alarm and took off. "Draw the curtains!"

"What?"

"Draw the curtains. Now!"

It swooped under the ceiling and flew around in agitated circles. Hurriedly, Seren tugged the dusty red curtains across the window until the room was dark and shadowy.

"Now lock the door!"

"I can't lock it! What's the matter with you? Do you recognize him?"

The Crow landed on the bed and fell over, then wriggled under the quilt, only its tail sticking out. Its voice came muffled through the thick blankets. "Of course I recognize him, you impossible girl. He's my . . . er . . . my enemy!"

"Your enemy?"

"Well, he took me apart and put me in newspaper, didn't he?" The Crow's jewel eye peeked wickedly out at her. "I don't want to go with him. Don't let him find me!"

Seren shook her head. She had no idea if any of this was true. Was the Crow really scared? She frowned and said, "All right. But in return, you come down into the cellar with me and we look for Tomos."

The quilt shuddered. "No chance!"

Seren turned to the door. "Then I'll go down there and tell him where you are."

"You won't," the Crow screeched, "and if you do, I'll make myself invisible, or I'll turn myself into an ant or . . ." It stopped.

Far below, the knocker on the front door sounded out. Three heavy thuds echoed through the house.

Seren smiled sweetly. "Well?"

The Crow lay flat and still under the quilt. "OK," it whispered. "It's a deal."

A GREAT BLIZZARD

Here's a globe of greenest glass
And a silver dress.

Seren waited at the top of the stairs, listening to the voices below. Mrs. Villiers's high, calm voice and the stranger's agitated one. She was worried. This would mean telling lies, and Mrs. Villiers would know and would send her back to St. Mary's.

The door opened and Mrs. Villiers came out, looking up and seeing her where she sat in the slant of moonlight. "Come down here!" she snapped. "At once."

Seren ran down.

The stranger was standing on the hearthrug of the blue drawing room, and all the furniture was ghostly under the white covers. As soon as he saw Seren, he hurried forward with relief. "Oh, thank heaven! It is you! I got your letter . . . I can't tell you how scared I was when I got back . . ."

Seren opened her eyes wide. "What letter?"

He was as thin and scared as before. "The one you wrote. That's why I came. For the Crow."

She took a deep breath and said quickly. "I'm sorry, there must be some mistake. I haven't got the Crow."

Mrs. Villiers's mouth made a perfect O of dismay. "Why, you wicked little girl! Of course you do. I saw it myself in your room."

Seren felt uncomfortable. But she had to face them and keep up the lie if she wanted to find Tomos, though the thin man's face was making her feel very sorry for him.

"I mean I haven't got it anymore. I put the key in and wound it up and it flew away. It flew out of the window."

"Oh, for heaven's sake!" Mrs. Villiers marched to the door. "I know exactly where it is and I'll fetch it now, Mr. . . . er . . ."

She left the room and headed upstairs.

Seren followed her and waited anxiously at the foot of the stairs. She could hear the thin man pacing the room. When Mrs. Villiers started coming down, she hurried back in.

Immediately, the man stepped forward. He took his hat off, and Seren saw his white face with its anxious blue eyes. "You wound it up?" He stared at her. "What happened then?"

"I told you. It flew. Out of the window. It made me jump so much!"

He was silent. Then he whispered. "Did it do anything else? I mean did it . . . speak?"

Seren kept her gaze innocent. "Speak? How could it speak?"

He looked at her, and she looked back, and for a moment she knew he knew, but he didn't have time to answer because Mrs. Villiers swept back in, looking hot and annoyed.

"Seren! I've searched your room and your bed and your wardrobe, and the toy is not there. This is ridiculous! You can't keep something that belongs to someone else, that's theft. Where is the thing?"

"I don't know," Seren said with perfect truth. She wondered where it was hiding.

"You must!"

"I don't."

Mrs. Villiers looked furious. "Tell me now!"

"I can't." Her voice was small but determined.

"That's it! I've had enough of your behavior here. I will have you sent back tomorrow."

"But—"

"Don't speak to me!" The housekeeper turned on the thin man. "I can only apologize, Mr. . . . er . . . for this girl's behavior. Leave it to me, please. I will get to the bottom of this. If you return at this time tomorrow, I assure you I will have your . . . parcel waiting for you."

The thin man looked as if he was barely listening. His blue eyes were fixed on Seren. Then, sadly, he said, "I think I understand what has happened here. Please don't punish the girl. It's not really her fault. I know who is to blame . . . he hates being taken apart so much, and he's so—"

"Punish?" Mrs. Villiers smiled icily. "Don't worry about that. Tomorrow, then. Goodbye."

She ushered the man out. Seren had one glimpse of his face, anxious and bewildered, and then he was gone, and the murmur of voices died away along the corridor.

She waited. She was really scared now.

When Mrs. Villiers came back, they faced each other in silence across the dark and cheerless room. "I have no idea what sort of person you are," the tall woman said quietly, "but I will not have a thief in the house. For the last time, where is this toy?"

"I don't know."

"I see." Her hands were knotted together in anger; she drew herself up. "Well then, you will go to your room at once without supper and you will pack your bag. Tomorrow, Denzil will drive you to the station."

"Tomorrow!"

Mrs. Villiers nodded grimly. "You will have a one-way ticket back to the orphanage, and I will write to Lady Mair and explain that her generosity has been wasted on a thief and a liar. And that is only what you deserve, you wicked, *wicked* little girl!"

A great sob rose up in Seren's throat. Suddenly, she just wanted to blurt everything out, that she was doing this for Tomos, that it wasn't fair, any of it. But she managed to keep silent.

Mrs. Villiers rang the bell, and Denzil appeared so quickly that he had obviously been listening outside.

"Take her upstairs. No supper."

Seren followed him out. Looking back, she saw Mrs. Villiers had turned around and was staring into the dull red coals of the hearth, her arms folded.

Denzil said nothing. The house was a great darkness. They went along its corridors, and the moon was slanting in everywhere, in lines and rectangles of silver.

Finally he turned and looked at her. "You all right, girl?"

"Fine."

"Wish I knew what you were up to."

"Nothing," she whispered.

"Wish I believed that." At her door, he stopped. "Keep your window closed and your door shut. There's a bitter coldness in the house tonight. An icy silence. I can feel it."

"You mean the Family, don't you?"

His face was dim in the candle shadows. He said, "Don't talk of Them. They have the boy, we all know that. All the spells in the world won't bring him back to us. We should have explained it to you, but we don't speak Their name now." For a moment, he seemed to forget she was there; his voice went dark and hoarse. "Dear Tomos. In what dark place is he? How I miss that boy. What Christmases we had when he was here."

Seren nodded. She said, "Good night, Denzil."

"*Nos da, Seren bach.* I will miss you, too. I was getting used to having you here."

She liked the way he said her name, *Star.* But she was not going anywhere.

In the room, she searched hastily, but there was no sign of the Crow until a *tap-tap* on the glass made her look up in alarm.

The Crow's jewel eye was pressed against the frosty glass. She ran and opened the pane.

The Crow tumbled in, half-frozen. "I cannot feel my feet!"

She peered beyond it, but the thin man, if he was still there, was lost in the shadows of the trees, where they lay long and blue under the moon. The lawns shone ghostly white under the stars.

The night seemed to hold its breath, cold and intent.

Seren went back and climbed onto the bed. The Crow sat in a shivering heap in front of the fire, small drips of water melting from it and making a wet stain on the rug.

"They're sending me back."

"Expec-c-c-c-ted," the Crow's beak chattered.

"How can I stop them? How can I make them keep me here?"

The Crow looked at her over one shoulder. Then it hopped over to the table where Tomos's diary lay and flicked the pages with the tip of its wing. "I was reading this. The boy's handwriting is a disgrace and he should have the cane for untidiness, but this bit is interesting. Listen."

In its croaky voice it began to read.

> Today I met a strange person in the lane. She was bent over like an old woman, and she had a basket on her arm. "Buy from me, young master," she said.
>
> I told her I didn't have any money, which was true.
>
> "Then take a present from me," she said. She held out a snow globe. How could she know I collect them! It was a really beautiful one. The

glass is green and thick, and there is an icy palace inside.

I couldn't resist. I took it, though I shouldn't have.

Seren stared at the globe. "This one!"

"Clearly." The Crow touched its beak, as if pushing up a pair of spectacles. Then it read on.

"Come and be a prince there," she said.

That made me scared. I just said "Diolch" and ran. When I turned back, she was going into the wood. But I think, under her hood, I saw long white hair.

And a silver dress.

It looked up. They both stared at the snow globe.

"Interesting." The Crow closed the book and tipped its head. "A magic object, perhaps. Something to tempt him."

"The other day," Seren said slowly, "when I shook it just a little bit . . ."

"It snowed. And to stop them sending you back, you need—"

"Snow! Lots of snow!"

She reached out her hand, took the snow globe from the bedside table, and, very carefully, her eyes on the dark of the window, she shook it.

In the small world under the glass, flakes swirled around the palace of ice.

And at once, outside the dark panes, the snow began to fall, harder and harder, not in a soft drift, but with the hard, sleety rattle of a storm, and the wind roared against the roof. In seconds, there were already patches of white that slid and built up on the window's lead bars. Seren dragged the blanket around her, padded to the window, and looked out.

The night was a great blizzard. The stars were gone, and the trees were lost in whiteness.

She climbed into bed and lay watching the snow fall and fall.

"Now no one can take me anywhere," she said.

DOWN THE GOLDEN STAIRS

The clock is gray with dust
In the land where time is lost.

For a night and a day, the snow fell. The house grew colder. Ice formed on the windows, and small birds came to the sills and pecked at the crumbs Denzil threw out for them. Snow banked up high against the doors, the branches of the trees became laden with it, and only tiny berries of holly were bright in a white world.

Wrapped in a shawl, Seren sat watching from the window of her room. There was no way they could send her back. No one could even get outside until late in the day when the blizzard finally stopped, and she heard the scrape of a shovel and knew Gwyn or Denzil was out there somewhere, clearing a path.

The Crow spent the time huddled up by the small fire

Mrs. Villiers had allowed her to light. It was a picture of misery. "I have never been so cold," it said, shivering.

"At least the thin man can't get at you," Seren said with satisfaction.

The snow globe stood on her table, green and glinting.

She dared not shake it again.

Finally, as darkness fell and the light from the lamp in the window sent a faint glimmer across the blue shadows of the snow, Denzil brought her up a tray of supper.

"We've cleared a path," he said.

She knew what that meant. Tomorrow, the carriage horses would be saddled and she would be driven to the station. But she just smiled at him.

He went away, shaking his head. She tried not to worry. Because at midnight tonight, the bell would ring. It had to! As it had for Tomos.

It was hard to settle. She wandered aimlessly around the room until the Crow muttered, "Oh, you're making my head ache. Sit still!"

Instead, she put on her old dress, put some of the bread and cheese from the supper tray in her pocket, and wrapped her shawl around her.

When the clock struck ten, she took some paper and a pencil from the bedside table and wrote:

Dear Mrs. Villiers,

I have gone to find Tomos. Please don't worry. I will be back as soon as I can.

Yours sincerely,
Seren

She put it in an envelope, wrote *Mrs. Villiers* on it, and propped it on her pillow. She climbed up onto the bed and lay back.

"Now," she said, "we wait. You keep watch."

The Crow snorted.

The bell woke her.

Instantly, she jumped up.

It rang with such a sharp, silvery urgency, she thought everyone in the house must have heard it.

But if they had, no one stirred.

The room was bitterly cold, and the world outside

a whirling spiral of snowfall. The Crow was asleep and snoring. Seren slid out and shook it, and as soon as it opened its beak, she pinched it shut.

"Shh! The bell rang! I'm going down there." She took a breath. "You're not scared, are you?"

Carefully, she took her hand away. The Crow spat out imaginary fluff and looked at her in disdain.

"I'm a prince. I don't get scared."

Seren grinned. "Come on, then." She grabbed her coat, struggled into it, and pushed Tomos's diary into one pocket. After a second's thought, she pushed the snow globe into her other pocket. Then she slipped out.

The Crow flew after her, a swooping shadow.

They hurried downstairs. The whole house was strange. Snow-glimmer lit ceilings and odd corners with a reflected whiteness; the clocks seemed to tick louder, and the eyes in the portraits on the walls watched them pass beneath. She felt as if the books and the furniture and the mirrors were all alive and interested. Doors opened easily, and no floorboards creaked. It was as if the house wanted her to flit silently through its secrets, as if it wanted her to find Tomos.

She tiptoed past the kitchen. The fire had burned

down, the ashes settled. She could still smell the faint remnants of Denzil's tobacco.

The cat, asleep on a stool, lifted its head and watched her pass, but it didn't get up.

She came to the top of the cellar stairs and began to creep down them. They were cold and damp, and her breath made great clouds. It was slippery, too, and scary, but she thought of Tomos pattering down here in his slippers and that gave her some courage, because only she could find him now. And when he came back, how Lady Mair would cry out with joy!

At the bottom of the steps, she lifted her candle high and looked around.

She saw a glow. A golden, shimmering glow.

It was coming from the adjoining cellar.

"See that?" she whispered.

The Crow said, "Yes. Very strange." It flitted through the arch. Seren followed.

The cellar was small and vaulted, and the light was so bright, she didn't need the candle. She placed it on the floor in its holder.

The air quivered, as if the echo of the bell still hung. And there, before her, were the golden stairs.

They seemed misty, almost shimmering, but they were real enough, and they ran through the wall and down into the floor. If she stared hard, she could still see the bricks and the stone slabs through them, but they were insubstantial now, faded to nothing.

She came to the top step and looked down.

The stairs twisted into a golden haze so she couldn't see where they went.

"What do you think?" she asked.

The Crow perched on the stair rail and tipped its dark head. "I think you're scared."

Seren nodded. She licked her dry lips. "Yes, I'm scared," she said, "but I'm not going to let that stop me." Then she began to walk down.

It was so strange! The steps weren't there, and yet they were. The light was golden, and it was all around her, but it wasn't warm. In fact, the farther down she went, the colder her heart and her fingers felt.

"Are you here?" she whispered.

"Right by you. In fact."

She felt the Crow's awkward weight land on her shoulder. "That's better," she said.

Did the stairs twist left or right? She couldn't tell.

But gradually, as she spiraled down them, the golden glow faded and became more of a flickering light, and the air grew colder and colder until she could see rock walls, glistening wet with seams of coal and quartz.

"It's a cave . . ."

She heard something. *Music.* It was far, far away, but it was so sweet, it made her want to both cry and laugh at the same time. She jammed her hands over her ears. "I can't stop hearing it!"

"Take this," the Crow said hastily.

It plucked one feather from its tail and held it out; she took it.

"Oh," she said, hugely disappointed.

Because now the music was gone.

"Keep the feather on you and you won't hear it."

"I want to hear it."

"Yes, of course you do, stupid. That's how they get you." The Crow sniffed and watched her tuck the feather in her belt. "So. Which way now?"

They had reached the bottom of the stairs. The tunnel divided into three in front of them. The right-hand one had walls of golden stone, the center one had walls of silver ice, and the left-hand one had walls of bronze.

Seren frowned. "How am I supposed to know?"

"Well, I don't suppose it matters." The Crow peered into the tunnels curiously. "Wherever They want you to go, They'll lead you."

"Left, then." In the stories, it was always the third one that was right, never the gold or silver. Her heart thudding, Seren stepped into the bronze tunnel.

It ran straight ahead. Her footsteps made a weird metallic clatter, echoing all around. She felt like that girl in the book, Alice, deep under the ground, where everything was strange. Especially when they came to the well.

It lay in her path, a round hole, all blackness. A ladder made of bronze rungs led down it, and the tunnel ended beyond in a solid wall.

"You go down first and see what's there," she whispered.

"No chance," the Crow snapped. It perched on the ladder top and gazed down. "Looks deep."

Seren shrugged. She knotted up her skirt, swung herself over the edge, and began to descend the ladder.

She went down and down and down, until there was nothing but darkness, and her hands were sore, and her breath was gone, and her own weight dragged at her.

She stopped, clutching tight, her breathing huge in the well. "It's getting smaller. The walls are closing in."

The Crow said, "Stay there." It flew down past her and was gone, deep into the dark. Seren waited, but it didn't come back. She couldn't stay here, hanging on, so she continued down, and after a while the Crow swooped up. "Not much farther," it whispered. "And then you'll get a big surprise."

Seren nodded. She was so cold, she couldn't speak.

But at that moment, her foot touched something soft. She had reached the floor.

To her astonishment, it was carpeted with green grass, so rich and thick her feet sank into it. Small white flowers grew everywhere, their sweet smell over-powering.

Seren stared around. She was standing in a meadow that stretched as far as she could see. The sky was blue, but there was no sun or moon, just a pale light that cast no shadows and never seemed to change.

Seren blew hair from her eyes and untied her skirt. "Maybe I should have taken one of the other tunnels. Where now?"

The Crow landed and looked closely at the flowers.

"This is so strange. No insects. No butterflies. The petals of these flowers look like crystal."

"That's not much help." She set off, walking.

The Crow hopped behind. "And I can smell something."

"What is it?"

The Crow stopped, considering. Then it said, "Danger."

The walk through the meadow might have taken hours or days, but there was no time here. Seren didn't even get tired. After a while, she realized the meadow was gone and she was walking through a wood. When had that happened? It was like being in a dream, but the wood was scary. The trees were all black, and their trunks contorted and tangled, and the farther on she went, the more tangled they got. It was like they were laughing at her.

At first, she thought nothing else lived down here. Then she saw a fox.

It sat under a tree and looked at her, its yellow eyes sly and alert. Quickly, it slid away into the trees.

"Oh dear. I think They've spotted us," the Crow muttered nervously.

A little later, there was an owl, high in the branches. Seren stopped and the owl stared down. It didn't fly away.

"I only want to find Tomos," she said to it quietly. "And to take him home. That's all."

The owl blinked.

Seren gasped, because it had become just an owl-shaped hole in the tree.

"No use talking to Them." The Crow was looking over her shoulder. "They don't take any notice. Anyway, look there!"

Seren turned, and at once a great cry broke from her.

Beyond the wood, high on a hill of snow, there rose a palace. It was like all the palaces she had read about in the fairy tales, diamond-white and shining. It had thin towers and turrets, high walls, gleaming roofs of silver. Every pinnacle was decorated with a flag, and each flag showed a different bird—owls, eagles, ravens.

"No crows," the Crow said in disgust. "Snobs."

Annoyed, it flew straight toward the palace, and then suddenly, with a great *smack*, it bounced backward and fell into the dark grass.

Seren raced toward it. "Are you all right?"

The Crow was dazed. It lay on its back. For a moment, it stared, its eyes blank, then it blinked twice and sat up. Its beak was even more dented than before, and it looked furious.

"I should have known!"

"What?"

"Can't you feel it? Just reach out! Feel it! I could have broken my neck!"

Seren did, putting her hand out cautiously into thin air. She touched something hard and smooth and invisible, and as she felt along it, she found that it rose up and out as far as she could reach in any direction: a great wall of invisible glass. She stretched up on tiptoe. But there was no end to the glass.

"The palace is covered with a great dome," the Crow snapped. "And there's no way through."

Inside the glass, it was snowing. Stars sparkled in the sky. One window, high in the palace, had a light inside it. Maybe Tomos was up there, a prisoner. But how could they reach him?

Seren put her palms flat against the glass and her nose against it and stared in.

"It's an enormous snow globe!" she whispered.

THE PALACE OF ICE

Walls of ice, stars of silver.
Winter ways you'll walk forever.

t's impossible." Finally Seren had to stop for breath. She stared ahead in despair. "There's just no way through!"

She had tramped along the outside edge of the invisible globe for what had seemed like hours, the Crow fluttering above her, but the strange thing was that nothing changed or moved. Inside the glass, the palace still stood tall and glittering, and the snow still fell soft and silent, while out here stars were scattered like diamond dust in a black velvet sky.

She didn't feel tired, but she was starting to get seriously annoyed.

"Typical of Them." The dent in the Crow's beak made

it sound even testier. Seren had tried to straighten it, but the Crow had pecked her fingers away and snapped, "Leave it! I'll survive!"

Now it swooped down onto the grass in front of her.

"What do you mean?" she said.

"I mean They're laughing at us. We're wasting our time."

"I thought time was different here?"

"You know what I mean!" The Crow shook its head. "If there's really a way through, we won't find it walking in circles."

"There must be a way. A door . . ."

"There won't be a door unless we make it."

"Why didn't you say so before?"

"Even a prince doesn't always get things right."

"But you always think you know everything," she snapped.

"I do. I certainly know more than a silly little girl."

Seren simmered. Still, she kept her temper and even managed a tight smile. She had to flatter the wretched thing.

"If anyone can get inside this glass dome, it would be you," she said. "I mean, an enchanted prince that knows magic. If you put your mind to it, I bet nothing could stop you."

The Crow looked surprised. It preened and smirked a foolish grin. "I'm glad you're starting to appreciate my talents. But it will cost me another feather, and I don't know . . ."

Seren made herself look small and humble. "You're so generous."

"Um . . . I suppose I am."

"And really clever. How will you do it?"

"Ah. Well." The Crow stared at the glass wall and the snowy world inside it. "Let me think." It hopped on one leg, then on the other, made a few rapid *kek keks*, and said suddenly, "There is one thing that might work, though it's tricky. I'll need a single drop of blood and a tear."

"What?"

"You'll have to supply those. Surely you can do that?"

"But what if it doesn't work?"

The Crow shrugged. "What have you lost? A drop of blood."

Seren scowled. "You're not the one who gets hurt." But she unpinned a small brooch on her coat, took a glove off, and, taking a deep breath, jabbed the point into her thumb and squeezed. A tiny drop of blood welled up. It hurt so much, the pain brought a tear to her eye.

"That's good," the Crow said hastily. "Now. Drop it here, on the glass."

Seren came close to the invisible wall and shook her hand. The small red drop fell on the glass and ran down.

"Now the tear." The Crow pointed with its wing. "Just there, please."

Seren put a finger under her eye and caught the tear. She carried it carefully and let it drip onto the glass.

Her thumb throbbed; she shoved her hand deep in her pocket.

Then she stared. The blood became a red line on the glass. It was etched like acid, and as she watched, it did the impossible and ran upward and then across and down, forming the narrowest of doorways.

The tear, where it hung, became a small, glittering keyhole.

The Crow watched her astonishment. "Impressed?"

"Yes! But . . ."

"A door of blood and tears." It stuck its chest out,

looking smug. "Pretty impressive, if I say so myself. It's a spell from an old grimoire I read once, though I have to say I've never actually tried it before. There are other interesting things in that book, too. For instance, if you want to change a snake into a river, you just—"

"What about a key?" Seren said quickly. She didn't want the Crow to get too puffed up; it was conceited enough already.

"Oh. That's my contribution." Reluctantly, the Crow shook the smallest feather from its tail, then uttered a sharp *karak* of command. The feather crackled as if a black frost had enveloped it, then she saw it had become a black key, lying there on the ground.

Seren snatched it up—it was icy cold—and slid it into the teardrop lock.

It fit exactly, and with a great effort, she turned it. The key made a strange snapping, clunking noise.

The door of blood opened. The glass shuddered and cracked apart, slivers of ice falling from it. A bitterly cold wind gusted out, lifting her hair, ruffling the Crow's plumage. With the wind on her face, Seren ducked through the narrow opening into the glass globe.

And sank into snow!

It was knee-deep, and so wet and cold, she had to tug her skirt up. "What now?"

"Walk. To the palace."

That was easy for a bird to say. Each step was an effort. The Crow fluttered overhead, the only dark spot in a white world of snowfall. Below, Seren struggled, lifting her feet high and staggering in the soft drifts. The snow was treacherous; it crunched under her weight, and its crusted surface glittered with millions of faceted flakes. Each step could send her plunging into invisible chasms or secret lakes; she had no idea what lay beneath. The snow stung her cheeks and clogged her eyelashes. She had to blink it away, but it kept coming. Twice she fell, her wide-splayed hands making deep prints in the drifts.

She was so tired! Looking up, she saw she was barely halfway across the snowfield. The palace rose above her, the single lit window in its highest tower. All she wanted was to stop, to sink down and go to sleep and let the falling snow softly cover her.

At last she sat, then curled up.

"What are you doing?" The Crow fluttered overhead in alarm.

"Nothing. Just taking a rest."

"Get up, you silly girl. Now!"

"Leave me alone." She was so sleepy and comfortable in the strange warmth of the snowdrift. It was like a bed, soft and white, and she thought there were invisible hands tucking her in and soothing voices whispering a lullaby in the wind.

She closed her eyes.

But just as sleep came over her, she felt something in the lining of her coat. A sharp corner was nudging urgently against her, and, sleepily, she knew it was Tomos's diary. As she thought his name, a new strength came back—a sudden wakefulness and warning—and she snapped her eyes open and said, "*No!* No, I won't sleep!"

She scrambled up, furious with herself.

The Crow looked relieved. But it sniffed and said, "They nearly had you then."

"No, They didn't," Seren snapped. But it was a lie, and she knew it.

Strangely, though, something had changed. The palace seemed nearer. With only a few more paces, she came to some steps and pulled herself up them. They led to a great wooden door, all caked in snow, with one large, round, iron handle on which the Crow was perched, hunched up with snow on its head. "Hurry," it said, annoyed, "before I freeze here."

Seren turned the handle.

The door grated open and they slid in.

It was so good to be out of the storm. She shook snow from her coat and hair onto the smooth white floor. Then she looked up.

At once, she took a great breath of excitement. A vast hall faced her. Its million pillars were delicate spindles of frost. High above, the roof was fretted with white lacework. The windows were tall lancets, the snow falling outside them. The floor tiles were solid slabs of ice.

A faint mist hung in the air.

Seren felt very small. She had left the wind outside, and it was very quiet. As she set out carefully across the great floor, her footsteps tapped in the silence.

"It's a palace of ice." Her breath made more mist in the air.

"Frozen solid," the Crow muttered. "Not my sort of comfort."

There were tables like slanted icebergs and chairs of spun icicles. As she tiptoed between them, they reminded Seren of something, and then she realized that it was the muffled furniture of Plas-y-Fran, covered in its white dust sheets. And here, too, there were pictures on the walls, but these were silvery faces in narrow frames, too beautiful and strange to be human. Their eyes watched her pass beneath with cold curiosity.

The Crow said, "The lit window we saw was up in the tower. So we'll have to climb. There are stairs over there." It swooped in a circle but then came back and perched on her shoulder, gripping with its clumsy claws. "Listen to me now, girl. This is important. They'll be here soon. They'll try to stop us getting to Tomos. If that happens, you keep going and you don't look back. You don't stop; you don't turn around for any reason. Any reason! Understand?"

She nodded. She had never heard it sound so concerned.

"What about you?"

The Crow shrugged, scornful. "Don't worry about me. I'm the prince. All right. Let's hurry."

They began to climb the stairs. The steps were wide and splendid, but at every turn, Seren had to step over a litter of objects. There was a rocking horse, frozen on its side, and a few steps above, a fort with the soldiers all spilled out and drawn up in rows, their tiny rifles pointing at her.

"They're his toys!" she said with a gasp.

"Mmm?" The Crow blinked its jewel eyes, glancing back.

"Tomos's toys! How did they get here?"

"How did *we* get here? Don't ask absurd questions, girl. Just keep climbing!"

She was breathless, half running past a scatter of clothes, a shoe, an open book—when she bent and tried to pick it up, it was hard as a stone and immovable in the ice.

A trail of jigsaw puzzle pieces led up the stairs as if they had fallen from someone's pocket. And the stairs were getting narrower, too, she thought, becoming like the ones at Plas-y-Fran, white and spiraling to the attic.

Then she saw the dollhouse.

It waited for her on the next landing. She had a stitch in her side and bent over to take a gasping breath, and she saw that the windows of it were all lit. Smoke was coming from its chimneys, and a tiny coach and horses stood outside it.

"Don't stop!" The Crow swooped past.

But she couldn't help it.

She knelt down, turned her head sideways, and looked in.

"It's real!" she murmured. "It's Plas-y-Fran!" And it was, because her huge eye at the window was staring into the blue sitting room, and the fires were lit, and Mrs. Villiers was there crying into her handkerchief at the table, and a lady was comforting her, a young lady in furs and a hat. Seren gasped, because surely that was Lady Mair—just as in her portrait, but her face white now with anxiety! And this must be Captain Jones, hurrying in with Denzil. Policemen followed behind him, and servants. Even Sam the cat was there, sitting on the mat. They were all talking, but she couldn't hear a word.

"What's happening?" Seren hissed. "How could they have gotten home? We've only been gone a few hours."

"Who knows how long we've been gone," the Crow snapped, circling wildly. "Time's not the same here.

Days might have passed back there. Now hurry!" It turned its head anxiously. "I can hear *Them*."

Seren listened.

Through the silence of the ice palace came a creeping whisper. A murmur of voices. As if a great crowd of invisible people was coming together from somewhere far away, talking angrily, and now she could hear footsteps, too, and hissing questions, and strange scratching, crawling, scurrying sounds.

"Run!" the Crow karked.

They raced up the stairs. The steps were steeper, more slippery. Behind them the sounds grew closer, but Seren willed herself not to look back, remembering the Crow's warning. Even so, out of the corners of her eyes she saw their reaching fingers, white as bone, their silver eyes. She gasped, her lungs aching, grabbed the steps, and scrambled up.

But where was the Crow?

"Where are you?" she screamed, not looking back.

"Go on!" Its voice was strangely croaky. "Never mind me. Get . . . to . . . Tomos."

It seemed far behind. And then, with a shock of horror, she knew that the clockwork was running down!

She stopped.

Instantly, hands grabbed her hair and skirt. She shrugged them off, yelling, "I'm coming back!"

"No!" The Crow's croak was harsh. "Get . . . Tomos . . ."

A whir of clockwork.

A long, slow slur of sound. "Ser . . . rr . . . rr . . . en . . ."

Then silence.

"Crow?" she whispered.

There was no answer. Seren stood still. The Crow had said her name. For the first time ever. And he was in trouble. She wanted so much to go back. But she felt *Them* all around her, Their hands on her spine, Their fingers in her hair, Their soft whispers in her ears. If she turned, she would see Them, and They would take her hands and They would lead her away, because already Their magic was in her heart and she longed to go with Them.

She took a breath.

Then she ran on.

Four steps took her to the top. There was a corridor,

its walls of ice, and walking along it, she came to the nursery door. She opened it and went in.

The room was a myriad of snow globes, and in all of them, a slanting snow was falling nonstop.

On a table lay dishes of food and goblets of drink, looking fresh and smelling so delicious, Seren felt her mouth water with hunger.

But in the center of the room was a huge four-poster bed, its hangings all white, and lying on the bed, staring up at the ceiling with wide blue eyes, was a boy.

As the door creaked, he turned his head.

Then he sat up and stared at her in amazement. "Who are you?"

Seren breathed out in awe. "I'm Seren," she said. "And you're Tomos."

THE HOST AROUND HER

Don't let them whisper in your ear.
Don't let anger keep you here.

If she expected him to be glad to see her, she was wrong.

He frowned. "I don't know any Seren."

She slipped in and slammed the door behind her. Soft fingers tapped and scratched on the other side. "I know you don't! I'm here to rescue you. Don't you—"

"That's just it," the boy said thoughtfully. "Where is *here*? I've been lying on this bed for a few minutes trying to work it out. It's like home, but it's not. As if They tried to make a copy and couldn't."

He was so calm! She shook her head in irritation. "Have you any idea what I've had to do to find you? All the trouble I've taken! And you just sit there!"

He was wearing a dark suit and boots, and there was a clear intelligence in his eyes. He looked at her carefully and said, "But how do I know?"

"Know what?"

"That you're real, and not just one of Their tricks."

"What?"

"Any minute now, you'll tell me to eat some of Their food. That's what They really want." He waved a hand at the loaded plates. "Look at it. All the things I like best—custard tarts, cream horns, eggnog. But I won't touch any of it, because if I eat it, They'll have my soul and I'll have to stay here forever."

Seren stared, impressed. "That's right . . . at least that's what it says in the books. But honestly, I'm not from Them. I'm real. I'm human."

"Prove it."

She came and grabbed his hand. "Does that feel warm?"

"Yes." He looked down at her rather dirty fingers. "All right, but . . ."

"And I've got this." She put her hand in her pocket and pulled out the diary.

He stared at it, then snatched it and riffled through

the pages. "This is mine! How did you get it?"

"I found it in your bedroom."

He looked up. "When?"

"A few days ago. At least . . ." She shook her head. "I think it was . . . I don't know how long I've been here."

He stuffed it inside his jacket, annoyed. "Have you read it?"

"Bits."

"You shouldn't have."

"I had to find you! You've been gone a year . . ."

His laugh startled her. "Don't be silly. Of course I haven't! I went for a walk this morning, in the snow. I ran down by the hollow near the lake and then I . . . well, somehow I was here." He frowned. "I can't quite remember how. But it was only an hour or so ago."

Seren shook her head. She grabbed his arm and pulled him from the bed, and he was exactly the same height as she was. "No, it wasn't! Listen to me! It was a year ago. A whole year. And your mother . . . all of them, they don't know what's happened to you. They say you're missing, but some of them think you're dead."

His blue eyes were hard with amazement, and then anger. "A year?"

"And a day."

"No . . . that's not possible . . ."

"Denzil says They can do all sorts of things."

"My mother . . ."

Seren could see he believed her now. She said quietly, "Your mother locks herself away in London. I suppose she can't bear it."

Her hand was tight on him. He shook her away. "How did you get here?"

"I went down the golden stairs you wrote about. And a . . . friend came with me, but he's lost. I think They've got him, because They've been after him for a while . . ."

Tomos wasn't listening. He had jumped up and already had the door open. "I'm going home right now!"

He ran outside; Seren followed him, then she stopped in astonishment. "It's all changed!"

Everything was different. There was no corridor outside, and no stairs, only a dark tunnel that led both ways into silence.

"You can't trust anything here. They play tricks on your eyes and your mind," Tomos muttered. He looked right and left. "Which way?"

"I came that way, but . . ."

He hurried left. "I can't believe it," he muttered, "about my mother. She'll be so afraid."

Behind him, Seren was silent. He thought he had only been here hours. How long had she been here? Was another year gone? A hundred years? It scared her, that time might be flitting past in the world out there.

They ran down the tunnel. Far off, cold voices laughed.

Ahead was a strange, bluish light. Tomos ran toward it, and Seren was right behind him, thinking hard. Where was the Crow? She couldn't go back without it, but how could she ever find it in this mixed-up place?

The tunnel grew narrow. Blue light shimmered. For a joyous moment, she thought they were coming to the end, but then the roof changed from rock to a mass of seamed ice, and through it the sun—the real sun!—was shining.

"Quick." Tomos turned. "Let me hoist you up. Maybe we can break through!"

He crouched, she climbed quickly onto his shoulders, and he managed to stand. She reached up and banged her fists against the ice slab of the roof, then splayed her hands flat against it. But it was so thick! There was no way of breaking it! And only a warped view of the world came through, the white snow drifting, the vague shapes of trees.

"See anything?"

"It's the lake," she whispered. "We're under the lake."

He couldn't hold her anymore, and she slipped, the two of them falling in a heap. Seren looked up, imagining how her hands must have looked from outside, banging silently and spread out under the frozen surface.

If only Denzil had seen them! There must be searchers out there.

"We could find something"—Tomos was looking around frantically—"and smash it."

"Maybe this." Seren grabbed a small stone at her feet. And then she remembered the Crow.

The stone dropped from her hand. "Wait. I can't leave the Crow in here."

"What crow?"

"It's a long story. But I wouldn't have gotten this far without him. He's my friend. He knows magic. We have to find him. We have to go back."

She turned and began to walk sadly back the way they had come.

"Wait!" he said.

"No, I can't. You don't have to come if you don't want to."

There was silence. Then she heard his footsteps running after her, and his voice. "Don't be sad, Seren. Of course I'll come."

She was so pleased, she smiled at him, and he smiled back. "I'm not afraid," he said. "Are you?"

"No," she said quietly.

The dark tunnel led a long way, out of a cave into a forest of tall trees under a sky full of stars. There was no moon and it was very dark. They saw nothing of Them, though behind every tree Seren saw shadows and felt eyes watching her.

Then, far ahead, she saw a small light through the trees.

Tomos stopped. "What's that?"

The light was a glint of red in the dark world.

"I don't know," Seren muttered, "but we'd better find out. Be careful."

They hurried toward it, creeping through snowy

undergrowth and prickly brambles, until they were close enough to see what it was.

A fire!

A strange, cold fire that burned without crackling, and all around it, fast asleep, lay a host of animals: weasels and foxes, stoats and mice, a badger, and many birds. And above them, hanging on the branch of an oak tree, was a silver cage.

Seren's heart leaped.

In the cage was the Crow.

It was all hunched up in utter misery, with its head under its wing, and the key in its side showed it had been wound up tight. But even when Seren ran up and grabbed the cage bars so that it swung wildly, the Crow didn't look up.

"What's wrong with you? It's me, Seren! Wake up!"

"I'm not asleep! Just fed up with all of it!" Its voice was muffled.

She stared at it in shock. "Look, I've found Tomos!"

Curious, Tomos came up beside her. "Is it really alive?"

"Go away," the Crow said, more distinctly. "Find a way back by yourself. I've finished with all of you."

Seren seethed. "You ungrateful little—"

"What have They done to you?" Tomos said.

The Crow was silent. Then it withdrew its head from under its wing and fixed them both with a baleful glare. "So you're the famous Tomos, are you! Well, this is all your fault! The torments I've had to put up with. My wings pulled, my key twisted, my shape shifted. And now I'm in this cage and I'll never get out."

Seren said, "But your magic."

"Oh, don't think you can flatter me into this one!" The Crow's eye was a flash of angry blue. "I've already tried everything I know. They've got me tight in here. And if I can't do anything, I don't see what an orphan girl and a silly little boy can do to help me."

Seren said, "Don't give up! There must be something . . ." But the Crow was already looking anxiously over her shoulder. "Leave me and run! They're coming back."

"But—"

"Can't you hear Them?"

Of course she could. A growing murmur of voices, a snow-crunch of footsteps. Tomos's hand grabbed hers. "We need to go!"

"Not without the Crow! And anyway, where can we run? They're all around." Her fingers tightened on his. Then, despite what she'd been told, despite the danger, she turned her head and she saw Them.

They waited in a wide circle. A host of tall beings, narrow-faced and silver-eyed, beautiful and strange. Their hair and clothes were the color of snow, rippled with blue and purple. Their voices were soft but harsh, like the cries of cats or the cold language of gulls. They called out to her, and she knew what They were saying, because it was her name, over and over.

Seren. Bright star. Stay with us. Come with us.

She stepped back.

The fire flickered, its red light on the Crow's eye and Tomos's hair as he drew himself up.

Seren! They called. *Why go back? No one wants you. No one cares for you.*

She clamped her hands over her ears.

Never be sad, Seren. Never die. Live here with us forever and ever. Be our princess, Seren. Be our queen.

"Don't listen to them!" Tomos growled. "It's all lies!"

But she was already listening. It was all right for Tomos. His mother and father were longing for him.

But no one was longing for her. No one would care if she never went back. The pale creatures smiled sweetly; some of Them sidled forward. Hands reached for her.

Come with us. Come, sweet girl. Come, silver star.

She wanted to. She really did. For a moment, it was all she wanted in the world. But she knew that Tomos was shivering, and that the sleeping animals were a warning. She stepped back, right next to the cage.

And then the Crow was peering through the bars, its jewel eyes right next to hers, its beak whispering at her ear. "I thought you were too clever to listen to Them."

"I am too clever. But you don't care."

"Well, actually, I do. Because you did come back for me."

She stared, and the Crow shook its head impatiently. "Oh, I know I'm a crotchety, testy old thing. All moth holes and mildew. But that's what I mean! No one else would have bothered. No one else would have rescued me from that newspaper. Only you."

It made her smile sadly. "I didn't think princes cared about orphans."

"Ah . . ." The Crow blinked uneasily. "Well, actually,

about that prince stuff . . ." It glanced at the crowding shadows, whispering close. "I'm afraid I haven't told you the . . . um . . . exact truth. You see"—it wrinkled its beak in horrible embarrassment— "You see, I'm not exactly . . . what you might call a prince."

Seren said nothing.

"I'm—well, I was, once—a . . ."

"Schoolteacher," she said softly. "I know."

The Crow's complete astonishment made her laugh. "How?" it snapped.

"I guessed. Probably because you're always telling me off."

Tomos glanced back. "Seren. They're so close!"

The shadow people had crept within touching distance. Their fingers caught her sleeves and her hair, Their fingers white and frail-looking as lace, but so strong. She squirmed and jerked back, but there were so many of Them, she couldn't pull away. Tomos cried out; Their hands were all over him, pulling him away into the crowd. "Seren!" he yelled.

She turned to face Them. It was all up to her now. She said, "I can't stay with you. I have to go back. I'm sorry."

Their smiles turned to ice. Their grip was a numbness of cold. Her hair was torn, They had her tight, They were pulling her after Tomos.

But one hand was free, and she wriggled it into her pocket and brought out the object that she had brought all this way, that she had kept safe, because it was the most magical thing of all . . .

The snow globe.

Tomos gasped as she held it up. "That's mine! A woman in a silver dress gave it to me!"

Seren nodded. "It's not yours," she said. "It's *Theirs.*"

All the Fae people's eyes fixed on it; They gave a great howl and grabbed at it. But it was too late.

With a scream of defiance, Seren threw it down on the hard ground, and it exploded into a million shards.

A DAUGHTER TO US NOW

In the joyful Christmas dawn,
Even stars can find a home.

The sky was black.

At first, that was all she knew, and that she lay under it, and it was like lying in bed, deep under a soft white quilt, because she was so warm and comfortable. Stars shone high above, and a sliver of moon.

It was only the Crow's voice that startled her.

"Are you going to lie there forever?" it croaked irritably.

Seren sat up. She was in a bank of deep snow. Tomos was sprawled facedown beside her, and around them, all the sleepy animals were waking and fleeing into the wood, the foxes with yelps of joy, the weasels with a scurry through the snow.

And there before her was Plas-y-Fran with its windows all lit up! People were running out from the house over the snowy lawn, a man and a woman, and behind them Denzil, racing as fast as he could manage, and Mrs. Villiers behind them, amazed, on the steps.

The woman was Lady Mair. She ran past Seren and swept up Tomos in her arms. She was crying out his name, over and over, just sobbing and sobbing, and she fell on her knees with her arms around him. The captain ran up and hugged both of them. There was so much emotion on their faces, Seren couldn't bear it; it was too much, and she looked away. Then she scrambled up in dismay because the Crow was lying scattered all around her, in bits.

Its wings lay in the snow, one eye peered out, and she had to search hard for the two claws and hurriedly gather up all the spilled clockwork of its chest. Its beak croaked, "Key . . ." before its voice ran down and the wheels in its chest creaked to a stop.

Hastily, she hunted for the key and found it trampled underfoot. She slipped it into her pocket, turned, and realized they were all looking at her.

Tomos pulled her close. "This is Seren. She found me. I would never have gotten back without her."

Lady Mair's face was streaked with tears, but she didn't seem to care at all. She caught Seren by both hands. "Oh, my dear, dear girl," she breathed. "How can we ever repay you!"

Seren smelled her lovely scent and felt the fresh warmth of her skin. She said, "I only . . . wanted to help."

"You have saved us all," Lady Mair whispered. "I will never forget that."

Screeches of delight made them stare. Denzil and Tomos were dancing around and hugging each other nonsensically in the snow.

"Seren." Captain Jones was looking down at her. His eyes were wet and he seemed dazed. But he said, "You are going to be a daughter to us now. I promise you that."

She was so shocked, she could barely answer.

It was all too wonderful to be true. Her joy was a bit scary; she almost dared not be so happy.

A voice behind her asked, "Did you really go there? Where They live?"

Gwyn stood there, breathless.

Seren nodded, looking at the snowy lawn and the

blue, frozen lake and the birds fluttering away among the dark branches. "I must have," she whispered. "But I don't even know where it was."

And then Mrs. Villiers came running from the house, all out of breath, her dark hair coming unpinned, and she knelt down before Seren in the snow and hugged her tight. Then she pulled back and looked at her.

"I'm so glad, Seren," she said. "And so sorry I was cross."

Seren smiled. "So am I," she said.

~

They told her she had been gone for a whole day and night. As soon as Mrs. Villiers had found the letter on her pillow, the house had been thrown into uproar. Denzil had ridden to the station with a telegram, and Lady Mair and the captain had arrived within hours.

Since then, the house and the estate and all the lands around had been searched, but nothing—not even a footprint—had been found, and they had despaired.

"It was so terrible," Lady Mair said later, toasting crumpets over the fire with a long fork. "You had vanished like Tomos, and none of us knew where. And then! Then we heard that sound. Such a strange sound!

Like a bell at first, a high bell ringing, and then an explosion, as if a ball of glass had shattered into a million pieces, and we ran out, and there you both were, lying in the snow!"

Everyone was in the kitchen. Tomos was cramming his mouth with hot toast as if he could never get enough of it. Mrs. Villiers poured tea for everyone, and Denzil just sat there, staring, with the cat on his lap. All their eyes were on Tomos, drinking him up, feasting on the sight of him.

Captain Jones came in and stood by the fire. He looked relieved and restless all at once. He said, "But what I don't understand is—"

His wife glanced up at him. "We will have the whole story. But not now. Not tonight."

He put a hand on her shoulder. "No," he said. "Because this is a very special night."

"I'm sorry your toy got broken," Denzil muttered in Seren's ear. "Let me have it and I'll put it back together for you, if you want."

"Oh, I can do that." Her eyes widened. "But . . . what day is it, Denzil?"

He smiled at her in weary delight. "That's just it,

Seren. It's Christmas Day. And what a Christmas it will be!"

~

It was already nearly dawn. Seren was hustled up to bed, though even when the door of her room was closed, she could hear Tomos and his mother talking softly as they passed up the stairs. What was he telling her? Would she believe that he had been in that enchantment for a year and a day and never even known?

Seren shook her head. She felt so happy and tired, but somehow sore, as if she had gone through a great, bruising struggle. All she wanted was to crawl into bed.

But there was one thing she had to do first.

~

Putting the Crow back together took longer than before. A few cogs were bent, and its beak was even more crinkled, as if the explosion had damaged it.

But finally she finished, and she wound the key and sat back.

The Crow groaned. "Oh, my poor head!" It shook out one wing, then another. "The agony of being in that ghastly cage! I'm all aches and pains. Pins and needles!" It flapped around and took a short test flight, then hopped onto the bedpost and looked down at her. "*Kek kek*. So. You did it."

"*We* did it. But not everything's right." She smiled sadly. "You're still stuck as a Crow. I don't know what to do about that."

The Crow sighed and wrinkled its beak. "You can't have everything, Seren."

She nodded and climbed sleepily into bed, then blew out the candle. Through the slit in the curtains, she could see the snow falling again outside, but now it was a soft, normal snow, not the hard glitter of enchantment, and it soothed her. Even as she fell asleep, she thought she heard, far off over the lake and the house, a shimmer of sleigh bells.

In the morning, there was a parcel at the end of her bed.

She wriggled down and opened it and said, "Oh!" in amazement, because there was the most beautiful dress of dark purple calico, with tiny pearls on its collar and bodice. And there was a shawl, too, of warm wool, with a fringe that swung as she whipped it around her shoulders and paraded up and down the bed in it.

"Look at this!" she breathed. "Look at it!"

The Crow's jewel eye fixed sharply sideways. "There's more."

Seren dived back into the parcel. Tucked in the depths of the starry tissue paper was a tiny box, and a note on it.

Dear Seren,

This belonged to my mother. Now I want you to have it.

Merry Christmas
Lady Mair

She opened it. Then she put it straight down and put both hands to her cheeks and said, "Oh my goodness!"

The Crow hopped closer and tipped its head sideways. "Very nice," it said greedily.

On the paper lay a silver necklace with tiny silver snowflakes all along it. Each one glittered, frosty and bright. Seren hardly dared believe it was hers.

"You might have been an orphan before," the Crow remarked. "But you're a princess now."

⌒

What a day it was! She wore her new clothes, and everyone went to church in the carriage, and all the people stared and murmured when they saw Tomos, and whispers went around the congregation like wildfire. And the singing of the service was so loud. Afterward, Lady Mair announced, "This evening, the Waits must come play music at Plas-y-Fran, as they used to, and you are all welcome to join us!"

Denzil wasn't there, and neither was Mrs. Villiers. To Seren's surprise, Gwyn was driving the coach. But when they got home, she realized why, because Plas-y-Fran was a house transformed, all its windows emitting a cheery glow, fires lit in every room, and not a white sheet in sight. Servants bustled everywhere. From the kitchen, the smells of pies and cooked meats and cinnamon rose. And as Tomos and Seren came into the hall, they both cried out with joy, because there, fresh from the wood, stood a huge Christmas tree, all lit with candles. Toys and ornaments and sweets hung from its branches. Angels and stars peeked from its top.

It was far better than the ones Seren had seen in the shop windows in London.

In fact, it was the most wonderful thing she had ever seen.

There was Christmas dinner under a chandelier glittering with candles, and then the town musicians, the Waits, came, so that the singing of carols rang through the house. Seren sat on the steps outside, listening, a happy grin on her face.

Until she saw, at the back of the crowd, the thin man.

She stood up. He edged through to her and took off his dark hat, and his face was worn and weary. He said, very quietly, "Where's my brother?"

She hadn't expected that. "Your brother!"

He nodded sadly.

Quickly, she led him away from the house and around to her window. They looked up. The Crow was on the sill, watching the carol singers. When it saw them, there was a moment when Seren thought it would dart back into the room and hide, but then it spread its moth-eaten wings and sailed down, landing on her shoulder.

The thin man said urgently, "I've been so worried about you! You have to come with me. I may have found a cure for you."

The Crow made an irritated *kek kek*. "I was just getting to like it here."

Seren said, "You can't stay under a spell all your life. You have to find out how to be human again. So, now, tell me the truth. Not that silly story about the witch. How did it really happen?"

"It happened," the Crow said stiffly, "because I was a foolish old man who thought he could be a magician. I found a book of spells and said one over myself. I wanted to be able to fly. Well, that came true! But then I didn't know how to get back, and it was years ago now, and the book is lost . . ."

The thin man held out a hand, but the Crow just looked at him darkly. "This is Enoch, my younger brother. He's trying to help, but he just makes more of a muddle. And I will *not* be taken apart and wrapped in newspaper again."

Enoch sighed. "Very well!"

"Promise?"

"Promise. But please, let's go. The train leaves in half an hour, and I've found a magician in York who might help us. Let's go, before *They* come."

The Crow karked a laugh. "*They* won't try anything. They've learned their lesson."

It looked back at Seren. And whether it was the magic of the night or just her own imagination, she never knew, but just for a moment, she saw reflected in the windows of the house a man with a thin nose and a sly smile and dark, twinkling eyes.

Then it was just a Clockwork Crow.

"Goodbye," she whispered. "I will miss you so much."

The Crow shrugged. It plucked out one black feather and put it into her hand. "Listen, girl. If you're ever in trouble, write a message to me with this quill. I will probably come . . . if I'm not too busy."

Seren grinned. She kissed the Crow quickly on the top of its head. "Thank you!"

"Get off," it spluttered.

She smiled and watched the thin man turn and trudge away through the snow, the Crow flapping over him like a shadow.

Above them, the moon balanced on the tops of

the dark trees. At the edge of the wood, the thin man turned and waved. The Crow sailed up and around and she heard its voice come back, faint and far.

"Behave yourself, Seren Rhys."

"I will," she whispered.

Behind, from the house, came an urgent shout. "Seren!"

She turned.

Tomos was on the top step, wearing a crooked paper hat. "Come on! We're going to play hide-and-seek."

Her eyes went wide. She had never played that. "I'm coming! Don't start without me!"

She turned and ran home.

Enjoy this sneak peek at

THE VELVET FOX

the second book in
the *Clockwork Crow* trilogy.

SEREN RHYS IS UPSIDE DOWN

Earth is up, sky is down.
See the world the wrong way round.

Seren's feet were wedged in the fork of a branch, so it was safe to let go with both hands.

She did.

Everything went giddy.

She was upside down, and fear squirmed through her stomach. Green grass—with Tomos sitting on it—swung above her head. Clouds drifted at her feet. She waved her fingers and dangled straight down.

"Look at me!"

"Be careful, Seren." Tomos sounded worried. "You're supposed to be finding conkers. I don't see how you can find them like that."

"It's great! You should try it." Her dress was knotted

around her knees—just as well, because otherwise she wouldn't have been able to see a thing. But now she could see Plas-y-Fran all topsy-turvy with its chimneys smoking and sunlight on the windows and birds on the roof and the front door opening and someone coming out . . .

"It's Mrs. Villiers!" Tomos hissed.

Seren gasped. With a great effort she swung herself up, grabbed the lichen-covered branch, kicked her feet loose, and fell into the heap of fallen leaves on the grass.

Breathless, she snatched a conker. "Where's the needle? Where's the string?"

Tomos grinned. "Don't worry. She's so nearsighted, she won't know it was you."

"Is she?"

"Yes. And she refuses to wear glasses."

Mrs. Villiers stood on the step, shading her eyes against the sun. She said, "Seren?"

Seren stood innocently. "Tomos is teaching me how to make conkers, Ma'am."

The tall housekeeper frowned. "Well, don't get that dress dirty. Strange . . . I could have sworn I saw something rather peculiar in that tree. Some great bird, flapping its wings . . ."

Tomos and Seren stared wide-eyed up into the branches.

"Nothing there now, Mrs. V," Tomos said quietly. Seren giggled.

"Don't sit on the damp grass." She stood watching them from the distance.

"Do it like this." Tomos pushed the needle expertly through the middle of the hard brown conker, pulled the string tight, and swung it around, making a soft whipping sound in the air. "See? Easy."

Seren frowned. Her needle was halfway in, but she couldn't get it to move forward or back.

"It's stuck!"

"Push harder. It'll go through."

She put the conker down on the warm stone of the step and forced the needle through with all her strength. It went right in—and the conker fell apart in two perfect halves.

"*Blast!*" she hissed.

"*Seren Rhys!* What did you just say?" called Mrs. Villiers.

.. * ⏝ .* *

Seren blinked. "Er . . . I said 'Rats,' Ma'am."

Mrs. Villiers shook her head angrily. "There are no rats in Plas-y-Fran, I can assure you of that!"

"No. I don't mean real rats." Seren felt flustered. "I mean, sort of—imaginary rats."

She glared at Tomos, who was giggling.

"Your imagination is far too vivid, Seren. I never know what you'll come up with next. Have you finished Master Tomos's birthday card?"

"Yes, Mrs. Villiers." Seren looked down at her broken conker. It was her third try at stringing one, but none had worked. Tomos had four already: fat, shiny brown missiles.

"So what do you do with them, exactly?" Seren muttered.

"Use them to smash the other person's. The one left whole is the winner."

She looked wistful. "That sounds fun."

Tomos laughed and leaned back against the chestnut tree. The sun shone on his brown hair and cheery eyes. "Haven't you ever played conkers?"

"There were no trees at the orphanage. Not many games either." In fact, she thought, all the games she knew she had learned here. She was dying to try this one. "Can we start now?"

"Not with mine!"

"But you're good at making them. Making all sorts of things."

"Yes." Tomos looked a little shy. "Actually, Seren, I've made you something."

He took something from his inside pocket and held it out, and she stared at it with delight. It was a delicate bracelet of red shiny beads all strung together, with a real acorn painted gold in the middle. For a moment she was astonished. "Oh, Tomos! It's lovely!"

"They're not real beads," he said hastily. "They're only dried hawthorn berries. But they look good."

She took it and fastened it on her wrist. "But it's your birthday, not mine."

He shrugged. "Well, I know. But it's just a thing to say that we'll always be friends. And on the back of the acorn, I've put a secret sign in water from the spring. S for *Seren*. It's invisible. I've decided that you can only see it when the full moon shines on it. That's my magic."

Seren couldn't see it at all, but she nodded, admiring

..*.⌣.*.

the loose loop of beads on her wrist. "It's lovely. It's the best bracelet ever."

He jumped up suddenly.

"Good! Now let's run!"

Restless, he sped away toward the lake, where a faint mist lingered. As Tomos raced into the mist, he seemed to disappear. Mrs. Villiers cried out in alarm. "Seren! Go after him. Quickly!"

Seren scrambled up. "Wait for me!" she yelled.

Tomos's footprints were dark outlines in the dewy grass.

For a scary moment, she couldn't see him at all. But then he was right in front of her, arms folded, looking annoyed. "I'm fine!" he snapped. "I'm getting sick of them all being so worried about me all the time. I can look after myself."

Breathless, she shook her head. "You can't blame them after what happened."

Last year, Tomos had been missing for a year and a day. The house had been an empty place of sorrow, and his parents, Captain Jones and Lady Mair, had fled in grief and bewilderment. None of them had known that Tomos had been a prisoner of the Fair Family, in Their strange underground kingdom of snow. No one except Seren—and the Crow.

"You don't know what it was like when you weren't here." Seren pulled a fallen leaf out of her hair and threw it down. "It was awful. So miserable!"

"Well, I'm safe now." He grabbed her hands and made her dance in a giddy circle. "And tomorrow is *my birthday!*"

His yell was so loud that it sent all the jackdaws up from the elm trees in a chorus of startled cackling. At the same time, the sun slanted through and drove the mist away, and there was the house, Plas-y-Fran, the right way up this time, golden in the autumn light, all its windows shining and smoke rising in slim columns from its clustered chimneys. Seren stopped and stared at it.

She still couldn't believe she was living here. Sometimes, late at night, she woke up from a dream and thought that she was back in St. Mary's Orphanage with the spiteful girls in the dormitory. But then she saw the curtains of her bed, and the cozy room with its fire and wardrobe, and remembered that it was all right. She was at Plas-y-Fran, she had rescued Tomos,

..*⸜⸝..*⸜

and she had a family. Now she stared up at the gables of the house and nodded firmly. This was home now. No one would ever send her away again.

A whoop of delight came from behind her.

Tomos had found a pile of red and golden leaves as high as his head. He kicked them wildly; he spread his arms and dived in headfirst. "Come on, Seren!"

She jumped after him. At once they were pelting each other with fistfuls, and there were leaves in her hair and eyes and even stuffed down her collar so that she screeched and pulled them out. Tomos tossed armfuls into the air. "I'm safe! They will never get me now! Never!"

As soon as he yelled the words, a gust of cold wind came out of nowhere. It whipped the leaves, scattering them like red rags over the grass, flinging them angrily aside.

Seren shivered. It was a strange, icy wind. It smelled of danger.

"Tomos, I don't think you should—"

"We beat the Fair Family, Seren!" He laughed as the leaves fell on his upturned face. "You and me and the Crow! We're safe from Them now! *Safe*. Forever!"

⋆*.. ◝ *..

The wind lifted the leaves. They swirled in strange patterns high into the air. A vast arc of them gusted down the driveway and past the gate.

And Seren blinked. For the red and copper and golden leaves shimmered and transformed, condensing and clotting into a strange, glistening mass; it became a red carriage with four wheels and two bright chestnut horses, galloping toward her out of the swirl.

"*Hey!*"

The furious yell came from a very small man who had come around the corner of the house with a broom and a wheelbarrow. "Stop that right now!" he roared. "Standing there shouting about Them. Defying Them! Why would you do such a thing, boy?"

Tomos dropped a guilty handful of leaves. "Sorry, Denzil . . . But They can't hear me . . . "

"Of course They can! Haven't I taught you better than that?" Denzil stabbed a finger at the woods. "The Fair Family are everywhere. Hiding, listening, spying, watching. In holt and hollow, bark and brake." He stepped closer, and some of the anger went out of him. Seren saw he was really very afraid. "Tomos, boy, you don't taunt Them. Never."

.·*·)·.*·

Seren took the handles of the wheelbarrow and pulled it closer, though it was heavy. She began to pile leaves inside, great rustling wet handfuls of amber and gold, while Tomos swept the rest together. But over his shoulder, she saw that the red carriage that had come so strangely out of the swirl of leaves was now rumbling toward the front of the house. The icy wind had gone as quickly as it had come; it seemed only she had noticed it. But it left a worry inside her. Tomos shouldn't have shouted like that. He was so restless today!

Denzil turned quickly. "Who's this then? Never seen that rig before."

Captain Jones had come out of the house. He stood waiting.

"Visitors," Tomos muttered. "Come on." He dropped the broom and hurtled across the grass. Seren raised her eyebrows at Denzil and then ran after Tomos, leaving the wheelbarrow half filled.

They reached the front steps just as the carriage rolled to a halt, the horses proud and whickering. Seren wanted to pat their soft noses, but she didn't have time because the driver, a small man in a scarlet hunting coat, jumped down and opened the door.

He reached in and a hand wearing a red velvet glove reached out and took his.

The carriage dipped. A large lady climbed out of it. She wore a traveling cloak and muff, and her dress was as russet and shiny as the leaves. As she looked up, Seren saw she had a plump, round face, with small bright eyes and frizzy hair pinned back in a bun. On her hair perched a tiny hat.

"Oh, my dears!" she said. "What a wonderful house! What a palace!"

She shook out her skirts; the fabric was creased and shimmery. "Such a journey I've had! Those trains . . . so comfy and warm. And I was quite spoiled with the First Class ticket you sent me, *dear* Captain Jones."

Captain Jones frowned. He looked a little confused. "I sent you? I'm sorry, I don't . . ."

"I'm Mrs. Honeybourne." She smiled and took his hand with her gloved fingers. "Oh, but you remember me now, don't you?"

For a moment, Captain Jones looked blank. Then a sort of flicker went over his face and right through his eyes, and he bowed hurriedly. "Ah yes! I remember clearly now. We met last week, in . . . er?"

..*.⌣.*.

"London."

"Yes, of course! I hired you to be . . . ?"

"Tomos's governess."

Seren blinked. *A governess!* She hadn't been expecting that! But, after all, Tomos would have to go to school soon, and he needed to be made ready. Would she go to school, too? A small shiver of excitement tingled through her.

Tomos must have been startled, but he didn't show it; he was always exceedingly polite. He put out his hand. "Hello. I'm Tomos Jones. Welcome to Plas-y-Fran."

Mrs. Honeybourne shook his fingers with great ceremony. "What a sweet boy," she murmured.

"Well, yes . . ." Captain Jones turned. "And this is my ward and dear goddaughter, Seren."

Seren bobbed a quick curtsy. "Hello."

"Hello, my dear." Mrs. Honeybourne's quick eyes took in every detail of Seren's face and dress. "So you're a ward! Goodness me, I had thought you were the gardener's daughter, the way you were piling up those leaves. How very foolish of me!"

Everyone laughed, though Seren felt a tiny bit

annoyed. But now Mrs. Villiers had come out of the house again with Tomos's mother, Lady Mair, hurrying behind her, and there was a lot of surprised welcoming and shaking hands and asking about the journey. Lady Mair said she had had no idea a governess was coming, and Captain Jones was very apologetic, and said how could he have forgotten, and Mrs. Honeybourne's trunk had to be pulled down from the carriage and all her bags carried in.

Seren said quietly to Tomos, "This'll mean lessons. No more conkers."

He shrugged. "It could have been a lot worse. She looks fun, actually."

Seren nodded. She had read enough stories about children being beaten and scolded by vinegary governesses to agree. Mrs. Honeybourne would be nice, she decided. They would have fun reading in the schoolroom upstairs about history and kings and far-off countries and wild animals, and maybe they'd do music and drawing. Tomos was very good at drawing. Much better than she was. And she'd always wanted to learn Latin and Greek and French and all sorts of things . . .

.. * ⌣ .* *

A large, soft bag was suddenly dumped in her arms. "That's my knitting, dear," Mrs. Honeybourne whispered. "Take care of it. I never travel anywhere without it."

"Do we have everything now?" Lady Mair said. "Then please come inside, Mrs. Honeybourne. You must be absolutely desperate for some tea."

They all trooped in. The table was set in the drawing room, and a small fire already crackled in the hearth. The room looked splendid, with bright china and glass in all the cabinets, much better than when Seren had first seen it, all dark and cold and the furniture under dust sheets. The whole house was alive now, and she felt proud of it.

Mrs. Honeybourne sank thankfully on the sofa. She took off her hat, and her hair frizzed out, but she kept her red gloves on. She stared around. "Oh, my lady, what a beautiful room. Such elegance. Such lovely china!"

"It was my mother's wedding set." Lady Mair poured out tea and handed it around; Seren liked the way she never expected the servants to do that. "We are so glad you've come, Mrs. Honeybourne. My husband tells me you are just the right person for our children."

Seren's eyes lit up. Our *children*! Just hearing that made her happy.

"Yes, my lady, and I know this is the right place for me." Mrs. Honeybourne drank a scalding mouthful.

There was a slight awkward pause. Then Captain Jones said brightly, "Well, I'll just leave you all to chat," and escaped through the door.

Mrs. Villiers said, "I'll prepare a room, my lady."

"Yes, of course."

When they were gone, Lady Mair put her arms around Tomos. "We are so proud of our children, Mrs. Honeybourne. Tomos is a great artist and Seren . . . well, Seren is such a reader! I think she's gone through half the library already."

"Already?" Mrs. Honeybourne's bright eyes fixed on Seren.

"I've only been here since Christmas," Seren said reluctantly.

"Really! And before that?"

"The orphanage."

"Oh, you poor dear," Mrs. Honeybourne said softly. "How terrible for you."

.·*∪.*·

Seren shrugged. "It was all right."

"So brave!" Mrs. Honeybourne finished her tea and rattled the cup into the saucer. "I will be teaching both the children then, Lady Mair?"

"Oh yes." Lady Mair nodded firmly. "We want Seren to benefit. We believe that girls should have as good an education as possible."

The governess smiled cozily at Seren. "Dear Tomos will need his Latin and Greek."

"I can do that, too," Seren said quickly.

Mrs. Honeybourne didn't answer. Instead, she squirmed around and began rummaging in the bags, wisps of hair coming undone from her bun. "I have something special for Tomos. Now where did I put it . . . I'm such a scatterbrain . . . Ah, yes!"

From the largest bag, she carefully lifted out a gold-colored box. "I know it's not until tomorrow"—she turned to Tomos—"but as soon as I saw this in the shop window in London, I simply couldn't resist it! Happy birthday, dear Tomos!"

She put the box in his hands.

Startled, he looked down at it.

"What do you say?" Lady Mair whispered.

★ *. ◟ *. .

"Thank you! I mean, thank you very much, Mrs. Honeybourne."

The box shimmered in the sunlight, an enticing golden cube. "Can I open it?"

"You shouldn't until tomorrow," Seren said.

"Oh, do let him." Mrs. Honeybourne clasped her gloved red fingers tight. "Just this once. I so want to see his happy little face!"

Lady Mair smiled. "Mrs. Honeybourne, you really shouldn't have bought anything. Tomos is quite spoiled enough as it is. But I suppose, just this once . . ."

Instantly, Tomos tugged the lid off the box. Seren stepped closer, craning her neck to see. Even Lily the housemaid, clearing the cups, glanced over curiously.

Tomos stared inside. For a moment his eyes were wide with surprise. Then he almost whistled with delight. "That's amazing," he breathed.

He reached into the box, carefully pulled out a large drum-shaped object, and put it on the tea table.

"Oh," Lady Mair said, clasping her hands.

"I knew you'd love it," Mrs. Honeybourne murmured.

"That's lovely, that is," Lily said.

.. * ᴕ .* *

Seren stared at it, astonished.

She had seen pictures of them in books. Though she had never been to a fairground, she knew what this was called.

A carousel.

Its base was red and gold, and in its center was a striped pole topped by a golden ball. The ones she had seen in pictures had all had wooden horses that rose and fell, for children to ride on. This one was far too small to ride on, of course. It had just three galloping horses, and each horse had a rider.

Tomos reached out and turned the small handle on the side, and with a faint, magical tinkling music, the carousel began to spin around. And the figures moved. There was a soldier in a red tunic who pattered on his drum as he rode. A dancer in a white dress swirled her perfectly pointed feet. A juggler threw glinting balls into the air and deftly caught them again. And, in the center, not riding at all but curled up watching them all with its sharp eyes, sat a small red fox.

"It's fantastic!" Tomos was beside himself with excitement. "It must have cost so much!"

* *. ⌣ *..

Mrs. Honeybourne smiled comfortably. She reached out and patted his hair with her gloved hand. "Worth every penny, dearie," she said.

Then she levered herself out of the chair and gathered her cloak and hat. "Well, I must go and find my room, my dears. Come along."

Piling themselves with her belongings, Lady Mair and Seren stood, but Tomos stayed with the carousel as if he couldn't bear to leave it, winding it up again as soon as it tinkled to a halt. The governess smiled and swept out into the hall till she came to the stairs. Seren, hurrying close behind with the bag of knitting, looked up and saw Sam.

The white cat was sitting on the landing, as if he'd come to inspect the new arrival.

Mrs. Honeybourne paused. It was only the tiniest fraction of a pause, but at the same moment, the cat opened his eyes wide, fluffed his fur out like a puffball, flattened his ears, and spat.

Then he fled in panic up the stairs.

"Why did he do that?" Seren wondered out loud.

Mrs. Honeybourne gave Seren a swift, sidelong look with her sharp eyes, and, just for a moment, the

..*.)..*.

governess looked like a very different person, angled and slanting in the mirror on the wall.

"Cats are such silly animals," she said.

Then she gave the jolliest of laughs, so that Lady Mair laughed, too, and they walked up the stairs together.

But Seren stayed on the bottom step, her arms full of knitting and a sewing box. *No, they're not,* she thought, staring after Sam. *Cats are clever.*

Then they called her and she had to run after them, scattering wool and needles.

ABOUT THE AUTHOR

CATHERINE FISHER is the *New York Times* best-selling author of *Sapphique* and *Incarceron*. An acclaimed novelist and poet, she has written many fantasy books for young people, including the Oracle Prophecies series. In 2011, she was appointed the inaugural Young People's Laureate for Wales. Catherine Fisher lives in Wales.